THE RAREST FRUIT

ALSO BY

GAËLLE BÉLEM

There's a Monster Behind the Door

Gaëlle Bélem

THE RAREST FRUIT

OR THE LIFE OF EDMOND ALBIUS

*Translated from the French
by Hildegarde Serle*

Europa
editions

Europa Editions
27 Union Square West, Suite 302
New York NY 10003
www.europaeditions.com
info@europaeditions.com

This book is a work of fiction. Any references to historical events,
real people, or real locales are used fictitiously.

Copyright © Éditions Gallimard, Paris, 2023
First publication 2025 by Europa Editions

Translation by Hildegarde Serle
Original title: *Le Fruit le plus rare*
Translation copyright © 2025 by Europa Editions

All rights reserved, including the right of reproduction
in whole or in part in any form.

Library of Congress Cataloging in Publication Data is available
ISBN 979-8-88966-099-6

Bélem, Gaëlle
The Rarest Fruit

Cover design by Ginevra Rapisardi

Cover image: Alston, Hooker, Trimen,
A hand-book to the flora of Ceylon (Plate XCI)/Wikimedia

Prepress by Grafica Punto Print – Rome

Printed in the USA

CONTENTS

1. EDMOND
Sainte-Suzanne, beginning of the 19th century - 17

2. EDMOND DISCOVERS BOTANY
Ferréol's garden, 1833 - 29

3. EDMOND DISCOVERS THE GENESIS OF PLANTS
Garden of Eden, golden age - 34

4. EDMOND, BOTANIST AND DISSIDENT
Ferréol's drawing room, a stormy evening - 39

5. FERRÉOL BELLIER-BEAUMONT
Bellevue neighborhood, end of the 18th century - 45

6. MONSIEUR ET MADAME DEJEAN
Quartier-Français, 1823 - 52

7. EDMOND AS SEEN BY VOLCY-FOCARD
Memories and *Notice*, 1830-1840 - 57

8. CHARLES MORREN
Belgium, 1837 - 61

9. HERNÁN CORTÉS
Mexico-Seville, 16th century - 63

10. THE VANILLA FLOWERS
Bellevue, 1837-1840 - 71

11. FRUITLESS ATTEMPTS
1841, *annus horribilis* - 75

12. *VANILLA PLANIFOLIA*
1841, a lucky year - 79

13. EDMOND TELLS FERRÉOL
THE INCREDIBLE NEWS
The vanilla nursery, late 1841 - 86

14. FERRÉOL AS PATIENT
The sickbed, 1842 - 91

15. THE BELLIER-BEAUMONTS
From Burgundy to Sainte-Suzanne, 17th-19th century - 96

16. THE SPREADING OF THE NEWS
Bourbon, 1842 - 101

17. EDMOND ON TOUR
Côte-au-Vent, 1843 - 105

18. EXOTIC VANILLA VS COLONIAL VANILLA
Atlantic coast, middle of the 19th century - 109

19. MONSIEUR BEAUMONT
The pinnacle, middle of the 19th century - 115

20. EDMOND AND ICARUS
High, very high - 118

21. No No No
The slaves' hut, 1843-1848 - 121

22. The Great Names Charade
Town hall of Sainte-Suzanne, November 22, 1848 - 124

23. Edmond and Sarda Garriga
Place du Gouvernement, known as Place du Barachois
December 20, 1848 - 128

24. Edmond Hits Rock Bottom
The bottom of a hole, 1849-1850 - 134

25. Edmond as Cook
Rue du Four-à-Chaux, Saint-Denis, 1851 - 138

26. Edmond Gets a Prison Sentence
Jailhouse on Rue du Conseil,
Saint-Denis, 1851-1852 - 144

27. Edmond Gets Out of Jail
The north of the island of Bourbon, 1852-1855 - 148

28. Edmond Becomes a Grower
Sainte-Suzanne, 1855-1862 - 155

29. Antoine Louis Roussin, Lithographer
Artist's studio, 1862-1863 - 159

30. Claude Richard
Jardin du Roy, 1862 - 163

31. The Meeting of Edmond
and Marie-Pauline Bassana
Commune-Carron, 1869 - 167

32. EDMOND'S FATHER-IN-LAW
India, 19th century - 174

33. THE WEDDING OF EDMOND AND MARIE-PAULINE BASSANA
Green room, 1871 - 176

34. THE YEARS OF MOURNING
Sainte-Suzanne, 1876-1880 - 182

35. THE END OF EDMOND
The Sainte-Suzanne hospice - 186

ABOUT THE AUTHOR - 191

Z. for the future.
Ours that you embody,
yours that you're building.
M. G. A.

Florebo quocumque ferar.
I will flourish wherever I go.

THE RAREST FRUIT

1

EDMOND
Sainte-Suzanne, beginning of the 19th century

*"At that time, this little Black creole boy, a slave of my sister's,
was my darling, and constantly with me."*
—Letter from Ferréol Bellier-Beaumont
to the magistrate of Sainte-Suzanne, 1861[1]

O n the day that Edmond turned up in the neighborhood of Bellevue, he knew nothing about botany or the Bellier-Beaumonts. Ferréol Bellier-Beaumont's wife, Angélique, had been dead for almost two years, and the entire house had died with her. Inside, life had slowed right down and the atmosphere was leaden. In dark, musty-smelling rooms, the specter-like servants muttered about the interminable mourning and the sad ghost haunting corridor and barn. Cobwebs wide as curtains veiled the windows, a layer of pearl-gray dust shrouded the furniture. Outside, wild grasses were taking over the five steps of the perron, which faced, in one direction, the resolutely closed door, and in the other, a plain bordered by forests and ravines.

After four years of a difficult marriage, this widowerhood might have seemed like a release. Quite the opposite: it had depressed the slaves and silenced Ferréol, a sallow strip of bark, aged thirty-seven, who now uttered barely two sentences every three days.

On the day that Edmond turned up outside the Beaumonts' creole villa, he didn't know he was in Sainte-Suzanne, a village less than two centuries old, with a local policeman and six hundred colonists, who called it a town out of a sheer love of hyperbole.

Edmond didn't even know that the year was 1829, and that

---

[1] *Archives de Bourbon no. 10.*

the greatest part of his future would play out in that very town, from that very moment, on a tract of land planted with sugarcane and coffee, lit up at night by a clay-colored moon.

A cyclone had just swept over the island of Bourbon.

Ferréol Beaumont's fields of corn were ruined, his estate devastated, the anonymous huts kneeling down below engulfed. But Edmond crossed the grounds, the vast waterlogged garden and the avenue of leaning coconut palms, without taking notice of anything at all. Iron gate staved in, crosses and gravestones toppled, columns cracked, *lambrequins* torn off, he didn't see them. Orchids upended, their tender green stalks sticking up, their blossoms down, Edmond didn't spot them. Flooded living room, damp bedrooms, Edmond didn't even open his eyes as he passed through them.

Edmond is just a few weeks old, a black orphan placed into Ferréol's hands one Sunday morning, because it's a Mass day and you don't abandon a child after a sermon. Much less, the day after a cyclone. Edmond has clean clothes, a terracotta rattle, and has just guzzled a pitcher of milk. So the gloomy slaves, the mourning garb, the irrigation canals full of mud after the rain, they really don't matter to him. He flies over the maze of puddles, heading straight for his fate, happy or sad, with the fleeting thought that, in three hours, it will be feeding time again, and for happiness, all you need is a nipple. Ferréol Beaumont, on the other hand, owner of land that's now a lake, inconsolable widower, and obstinate botanist, doesn't view it like that. As soon as he sees Edmond, a slave just seven weeks old in the arms of another barely seven years old, he spits onto the ground, then lifts up into the gray sky this body of an orphan, who looks him deep in the eye.

"What's this, then?"

"This" meaning the ebony slave that, slotted between the arc of a pallid sun and his squinting eyes, affords him partial shade. "This" meaning three kilos and six hundred grams of

soft flesh, wrapped like a black lamb in a woolen cloth. "This,"
then, a living bundle of blatant trouble. And he opens the note
attached to its wrist.

From Elvire, your beloved sister.
A birth for a rebirth.

A gift from Elvire, that's to say, an umpteenth attempt to get
a moribund widower to smile again. Ferréol has a think, while
Edmond gurgles from the shawl in his arms. After a useless
puppy and a parrot so noisy he wanted to wring its neck, Elvire
is now trying this Negro companion! The minutes go by, the
silence endures. Has he really sunk so low as to be seen as some
sordid refuge? Ferréol ponders some more. Maybe. Later. Now,
no. His pain brooks no pity. It's self-sufficient. So, no. Out of
the question. No to this creature. No to adoption.

No, unless. No, except. No, but . . .

A "no" that, as witnessed by his steward, changes, drop by
drop, into a tiny "yes." Because Ferréol has an intuition that,
before his eyes, is not a child but a kind of heaven-sent sign, a
premonition of a possible balm for his barely healed wounds.
When it comes to slaves, he owns around twenty. Animals,
plenty of them. Nephews and nieces, quite enough. None of
them has ever had the effect on him of this little imp, who's not
even weaned. With a resigned expression, Ferréol calls for the
wet nurse Colombine and, scratching his head, introduces her
to the baby she will have to breastfeed.

"Until the next livestock market," he thinks it necessary to
add.

But that's not the main thing. That he can't say. She wouldn't
understand this business of redemption, this feeling of a second
chance. He speaks to Colombine without looking up, ashamed
and wary that she might suspect there's actually a heart there,
under all the excuses, coldness, and surliness he's labelled

"character" going on two years. He repeats "next livestock market," even though he swore on his life that, while ever he drew breath, never would the child go there. Colombine, with her thirty summers and breasts down to her navel, who's just lost her own baby at barely six months and twenty-two days, turns her watery eyes on Edmond with disdain, grunts a yes, then leaves to continue making packing bags out of vacoa leaves. She has no more milk or kindness left for today. He'll just have to wait until tomorrow. And judging from the bitter tone of his voice, the baby knows the milk will be at best sour, at worst nonexistent. The future's looking uncertain.

With Colombine gone, Ferréol moves his face a little closer to Edmond; he inspects him from bonnet to toe, in general, in detail. Edmond has a round face, eyes like java plums, a domed forehead. His face is chubby, his hands dance, his smooth cheeks are round as the stones of longans. Ferréol, a seasoned horticulturalist, patiently draws up the nomenclature of all his features as though for a new plant, a species he's dissecting for the first time: dark eyebrows, a plump little foot that gives him a kick under the chin, a Lilliputian hand that reaches for his.

He's surprised to find the thing worth looking at, to feel ready to treat him as if he were his own son. Maybe that's what love is; for twenty, thirty years, you conjure up the ideal being from head to foot, the color of their eyes, the contour of their hands, their temperament, their family, their homeland, their source of income—you won't compromise, it's precisely him, precisely her, or nothing—just to end up falling madly in love with the complete opposite, and begging the universe's forgiveness for once being so goddam stupid. That's at least what happens to Ferréol, who is smitten with a baby of fifty centimeters, forgetting women, money, raisin brandy, and no longer wants any role other than that of father.

In a word, Ferréol is lost. In a way, Ferréol is saved.

In his blanket, the thing of forty-nine days and a hundred-and-fifty feeds, with that ability of a child to think before being able to speak, to love without knowing how to say it, senses that the gods are smiling upon him. For ten seconds, he puts on a good show for his First Judgment. Almost holding his breath, he smiles with his eyes at the pair of eyes scrutinizing him.

Ferréol, who sees none of this childish intuition, who knows not the first thing about any child, because the harshness of life has made him blind and widowerhood deaf, plays with him for another few seconds. Even he, of severed heart, can't deny it: the thing has the sweetness of a watercolor cherub, with little fists plump as clouds. He stares wide-eyed and, for the first time in two years, Ferréol utters a second sentence in the space of a single day. Not really a sentence, rather a word. A "hello," coming from the lips of a man who had become nothing but clammy hands, bile, and deep sighs. The eight oxen and six slaves observing him catch a smile, to which none of his nephews were ever entitled. Hello, did he say? With or without a Burgundian accent? What does it matter? On this stony island of Bourbon, without electricity or a gas lamp, it's as unusual as a double rainbow, the beam of a lighthouse in the middle of the night, a half-day holiday other than Sunday afternoon. The cows stop mooing, the servants bickering, the steward barking, up and down the stony path.

"The master speaks? He says hello to children?"

In myths and legends, that's called a marvel, a miracle.

In this pragmatic 19th century, tasting of manioc and potatoes, the slaves just say, "*Oté, not' maît' lé d'venu fou*"—hey, our master's gone crazy. Crazy about a child without a name, without a story or a family.

In fact, Edmond had had a family, or something resembling one, but death, slavery, those usual misfortunes, had soon put an end to it. This was Bourbon, after all, a wilderness that the Ministry of the Colonies had transformed into a land of slaves, to keep the economy on a tight chain. They had hoped to find the beginnings of civilization, but were confronted with nothing but jagged mountains, at the foot of which sprouted, here and there, like warts, more straw-roofed hovels than *bardeau*[2]-clad manors.

Before the cyclone, in the Bellier-Beaumonts' barn, behind the bundles of wood and sacks of *ambériques*,[3] a slave named Mélise, a Negress who worked in the yard and was the property of Mademoiselle Elvire, had hitched up her skirt, gritted her teeth, and, with her body a triangle, had brought him into the world—him being Edmond, a pickaninny, wrapped by his father in a rectangle of sacking.

Here had begun the first act of an outlandish human tragedy, of which the curtain of blood would close only at Edmond's death, fifty-one years later. But the universe witnessed it: for all of one minute and forty-six seconds, Edmond did have a father and a mother.

"I have a son!" Mélise cried.

In Edmond's eyes, it was half a century ago, it was yesterday, it's today. Because his mother's voice still resonates like a church bell in his heart. But in her eyes, this new being represented too many emotions, too much suffering, lived and still to be lived. Hell never spared anyone for having gone through it with a child in their arms. So, she died as soon as she'd given birth, Edmond on her belly, the cord around his neck. Because it was still a time when mothers would die hemorrhaging as midwives, equipped with, at best, forceps, could but look on.

He still had the other one, his father, a certain Pamphile, also a slave. Misty-eyed from a mix of sorriness, happiness and

---

[2] A small tile made of wood or shingle, used to clad roofs and façades of creole houses.

[3] A small pulse similar to a mung bean.

sadness, Pamphile gazed at Edmond proudly, but also uncomfortably, that he was there, that he should begin his life with a tragedy. Then Pamphile disappeared. From Edmond's sight, from the world, from History altogether. Dead or a runaway, Edmond doesn't know which.

It's this double abandonment that maimed him from birth. Later, when he speaks of it, Edmond compares it to a scar that runs from his head to his heart. A scar both unique and shared, because there are, he says, tens of thousands of them here who are scarred, barely alive, born of no one and going nowhere. He says maimed, however, not killed, because this double blow didn't knock him out, just stunned him; when he opened his eyes, he had a bitter taste in his mouth, and a heart this big. As if his parents' hearts had combined with his own to form just one heart, a ginormous one, the size of a pumpkin. It will be quite enough for him to shift the world and nudge the Moon.

Edmond knows neither the origins, nor the precise identity, of his parents, as if they had just sprung up from nowhere, one empty, silent day. Slaves rarely leave any memories of their lives. How they met, how long their passion lasted, whether love even came into it, when, where, how it came about—he knows none of all that, apart from mere supposition. His name was Pamphile, hers Mélise, that's about it. He'd doubtless been conceived in haste, one Sunday beside the river, on a patch of *fataque*[4] or a hillside planted with blue-fruited vines. Certainly not on a mattress stuffed with horsehair, or even straw. He's a child created and born from a standing position, with all the discomfort of an unstable future. And this initial fragility leads him instinctively to vulnerable plants, those that, to stay upright, have to cling to a support, a stronger trunk, just as he

[4] A tall, invasive grass.

does. Edmond marvels at the Spanish moss—to him, it looks like an old man's beard hanging from a branch—but he also needs the bark-clad giants, the hundred-year-old tamarinds, cracked all over, which serve as a shield between him and the meanness of the world. He doesn't say it yet, but it's close to the epiphytal plants—or "air plants"—that attach themselves to the mango trees that he can think most clearly.

For years, he wondered what hope, what folly had made his parents believe that a quick embrace should have a future, and that future have the face of a child who would grow up happy on a dunghill. An accident, a premeditated act, Edmond doesn't know. Maybe Pamphile and Mélise had finally resigned themselves to the idea that the flames of this purgatory would never go out, that they'd have to learn to walk on the glowing embers, with a kid in their arms, like the coolies of Saint-André at the Pandialé festival. Unless Mélise, horrified by this pregnancy, had knocked back all the phials of ipecac she could, so as to spill her guts out, but despite that, the little bean he then was had been determined to sprout.

In fact, he doesn't even know who named him Edmond. No more than he knows the exact date he came into the world. His birth certificate, like his mother's grave, can't be found. There are some who claim that he was born on August 9, the same day, same month as his death. As if he were doomed from the start, as if the Grim Reaper were already pacing around his cot. They've got the wrong date, the Reaper the wrong target. He's a child without a season, but with a summery temperament. He's just like the cyclones: unpredictable, vigorous, and turbulent. And that's worth any sign of the tropical zodiac.

Maybe he was born on November 20, St. Edmund's Day, after the half-legendary, half-unknown English king, who was at the peak of his precocious fame at fourteen, and is almost always depicted tied to a tree. Maybe Edmond is such a rare name that his mother chose it to differentiate him from the anonymous and silent masses he'll soon be joining. Even if Elvire and Ferréol call him Edmond, maybe his parents had given him another name, more closely linked to that Mozambique they tried, by every means, to keep alive. All he feels is that he's a rootless blade of grass that grows wherever the wind carries it.

No one's child is everyone's child, and the newborn Edmond—public property, greedy as a gannet—flies from hand to hand, from flaccid breast to well-rounded bosom, sucking gluttonously on every nipple until, a month and a half later, Elvire Bellier-Beaumont declares him quite ready to serve as consolation to one in a sorrier state than him. And that's how he finds himself in the arms of her brother Ferréol, the day after a thousand storms. At this time, he knows nothing of his loss as an orphan, of his future as a grower, of the dog's life that awaits him—a dog already baring its fangs at him. Bourbon is just one more Maroon land populated by White exiles and difficult slaves, ninety thousand heads full of lice and ideas that jump about in all directions. Between the exiles and the slaves, there's his little baby face, unsuspecting of the scenario surrounding him, founded on the race for spices, the embryo of a barbaric society, the two paltry towns crossed by sugarcane carts, by stewards hooked on whips that crack, blood that spurts. To him, Bourbon is but the vacoa basket in which he sleeps eight hours a day, and shakes a rattle the rest of the time. He cries for milk, paws at breasts, thinking that if life boils down to this, he'll soon get used to it, and happily live six more lives like it. His existence is still a little bit of paradise at the edge of a burgeoning world.

Edmond grows fast. He remembers the smell of his mother, the sound of her voice, less and less. Sometimes, a flower in Ferréol's garden or the singing of a Negress breaks his heart.

It makes him shiver or feel dizzy, just as others might be struck by God's grace during Mass. This perfume of a white rose, this heady scent of frangipani, this snatch of a song that makes him feel blue, he knows them without actually knowing them, he's already smelt them, he's heard it before. So he's sure that when he was but the size of a seed behind a belly button, his mother breathed in this flower's fragrance, made up this bouquet, sang this mournful tune that links him to her, to her ancestors, to all ages of the world in which there are fields of sugarcane, Black slave laborers, cotton crops and vales of tears. It's their very own way of communicating, beyond space and time, a door that only they can open, that servitude, death, absence cannot close.

Edmond knows he's not a slave like the others. That he slipped through the net cast by destiny. That the *Code noir* that makes new slaves of the sons of slaves only half-concerns him. He's an adopted child, the black Brutus of a white Caesar. He owes his strength, his education, and his grub thanks to the clemency of a father who is replacing his own. It's predicted to end badly, like all stories of adoption, that schizophrenia is brewing, that the fire is smoldering, that the son will again kill the father, but no one knows with what weapon. At this stage, Edmond himself doesn't know that he has murderous hands. He's content to babble among a load of uncles and aunts, who have divided up among themselves, like a piece of fat, the lands of the Hauts de Sainte-Suzanne. There are Marie-Josèphes, Elvires, Louise-Michels, Victors, a François known as Jean-Baptiste, all more or less twins, partly growers, partly engineers, Ferréol's brothers and sisters. When they envisage a better world, they buy slaves, stirring into the same pot civilization, colonization, and plantation. Edmond finds them neither nasty, nor bad; they're ordinary folk born thirty to forty years ago on the right side of the equator. As for miscegenation, friendship between peoples, they don't think about them. No more than they think about the abolition of slavery. On this subject in general, they all say firmly but cheerily: we're having none of that here. It wasn't them who wrote the *Code noir*. They merely apply it. But they do forgive their brother, as a widower adrift, his caprice of strolling about everywhere with a darkie in his arms. One excuses everything of a dying man.

Edmond goes from one house to another, sleeps in a real bed with a feather mattress, has Elvire for a godmother, commander Grand-Marron for a godfather. He says *ti père*—daddy—when the other slaves say *not' maît'*—our master. He's not blamed for anything, but opinions remain fixed. God is white, Africa is black. Nothing to discuss.

Since he's not the age for discussions anyway, Edmond is content to crawl about on all fours, tries to stand up, wobbles, steadies himself. He totters along, falls down, gets back up, directs his first steps, and his first word, to Ferréol. He plays hide-and-seek with him when he's trimming his croton hedge. He eats the same gruel as the slaves, as long as Ferréol says he can. Otherwise, Edmond runs after a cow's bladder stuffed with moss, which serves him as a ball, a present from Elvire, whose tenderness is almost alien in this coarse century. He seizes happiness with both hands, laughs at everything and nothing, pulls faces more than he speaks when watched by pickaninnies who envy him his insouciance. If they don't just call it insolence.

When Edmond is bored, he fills the mouth of a lizard with water, making its membranes explode and propelling them to the four corners of Ferréol's field. When he wants a laugh, he makes a chameleon chew a quid of tobacco, making it roll onto its back, legs in the air. When he feels strong, he charges like a pirate, armed with a wooden sword, at the coconut palms, against which vanilla vines cluster. Somewhere in his child's brain, he's sorry for not being in the right place, for being a double misfit, an imposter in short trousers, but he tells himself that it isn't his fault. It's that of the precise mechanics of chance that made him grow up between two races, surrounded by the rarest of flowers. Edmond has the life of a little rascal, barely fearing Ferréol's warning shots. He tugs at hems, shakes the legs of tables and knocks things off them. He finally mellows after two hard smacks, and runs off to sulk beside the gladioli.

Let him stay there! It'll calm him down!

With a flower tucked behind his ear, Edmond turns to plant observation. The consequences are less perilous. And the one only he can call *ti père* told him that good children who love flowers will go to heaven. Heaven, that's where his mother lives.

2
EDMOND DISCOVERS BOTANY
Ferréol's garden, 1833

A short distance from a field of watermelons and voracious blackbirds, behind a door gray as a donkey, there was a strange garden that everyone called Ferréol's garden.

Edmond only enters the house at the end of the central driveway under three circumstances: to sleep at night, to shelter on very wet days, and when he's ill. The rest of the time, he lives outdoors in a daily frenzy of activity, scrambling through bushes and chatting to an imaginary friend, like all children of his age do. The slaves may have the same eyes as him, but they don't see the same things as him in Ferréol's garden. For them, it's just an orchard of shady trees, a green hell made up of mango, benzoin, acacia and jackfruit trees that they endlessly need to prune, lop, defoliate, before having to go and tackle the sugarcane. For Edmond, this garden is a palette of bright colors that he's been discovering since Ferréol started pushing him around in a wheelbarrow. If his *ti père* wasn't forever planting orchids, if he hadn't told him, one by one, their wonderfully evocative names, maybe Edmond's horizons would be limited to that sugarcane his brothers-in-exile cut and stack all day long. If he hadn't sensed the savagery of the world, the way ants sense rain coming and make provisions, maybe he wouldn't have ventured to the left of the manor, where Ferréol has established a vast nursery behind a wooden door. Standing in the tray of the wheelbarrow, Edmond points stubbornly at the little stick that serves as a latch on the small door they call the *baro*, and leans over to release it himself. In front of everyone!

Before his almond-shaped eyes spring up Pluie d'or orchids, with their tiny yellow blossoms, red amaryllis in the shape of trumpets, bright pink quill plants that look like racquets, Chinese-hat plants, the orange berry of the physalis, which Ferréol calls "love-in-a-cage," and Edmond calls "little tomato." Not far from the grindstone grow lady's slipper orchids, which really do remind him of comfy velvet slippers. Nearby, there are cattleyas with large blooms, soft as silk; even nearer, a pink Phalaenopsis, another yellow, another mauve, that plant marvel Ferréol calls the butterfly orchid and Edmond calls *zoli flèr-z'ailes papillon*—pretty flower with butterfly wings. The exploration has only just begun. Ferréol pushes the wheelbarrow up to the lemon trees, on which the faham, an endemic orchid, grows. Thanks to his *ti père* telling him often enough, Edmond knows what endemic means: it grows only here, on Bourbon. Ferréol suddenly stops, and Edmond watches for his slightest move: the botanist picks a faham blossom and attempts a conjuring trick he learnt who knows where. One moment the delicate white flower is there, being twirled between Ferréol's fingers. He cups it with his other hand. The next moment, it's no longer there, it has flown away, vanished into thin air, disappeared. Edmond stares, wide-eyed and open-mouthed. He looks under the wheelbarrow, lifts the smallest branch within reach of his little fingers, it's uncanny, must be white magic. Suddenly, here's the vanished orchid back again. Ferréol spots it first: behind the ear of the boy he calls his *ti gâté*—his little darling. The slaves hear laughter, a cry of amazement from that rascal in short trousers. Their necks straighten, they prick up their ears. What's going on over there then? Grand-Marron, all shouting and scars, scolds those with their heads turned. Back to work! Here's where real life is!

So, here we kill ourselves working, over there Ferréol turns himself into a storyteller. With a hand close to his mouth so the slaves don't hear, he tells Edmond about the great battle of Cour-Verte, in which the army of the ladybugs confronted that of the charging ants for the conquest of the orchids. It was well before he was born, back when the mushrooms laid down the law. And Ferréol lifts the wheelbarrow and takes his passenger to see one of the last surviving mushrooms. Since that battle, it has been hiding under a convolvulus. And so their next stop is in front of the blue dresses of the convolvulus plant, where Edmond points at some brown patches, crying out: "Naughty mushroom!"

As the journey continues, Edmond, from his metal seat, lightly touches a glowing red flower, the ginger wax, which he calls "the torch" because it looks like the scarlet flaming one that Grand-Marron holds at night when he's guarding the property, or running back to Colombine. Then come the white peace lilies, which Edmond only touches with his eyes because, contrary to Grand-Marron, Ferréol says that flowers are like ladies: we only really like them from a distance.

The further the wheelbarrow advances, the more that appears before Edmond's astonished eyes: eagle ferns, hart's-tongue ferns, aeonium black roses, bird-of-paradise flowers that are almost more elegant than the birds themselves, with orange crest, long blue-green beak, and stem extending like the neck of a flamingo.

To those are added some lobster-claws, snapdragons, a clump of lamb's-ear, parrot tulips, the tiny petals of mouse-ear chickweed, fly orchids, stars-of-Bethlehem.

It's a vast bazaar of scents and colors, abuzz with bees and in full swing around the wheelbarrow ferrying Edmond.

To add a little spice to the walk, Ferréol always heads for a dark and almost misty corner where a *Dracula simia*, known as the monkey-face orchid, climbs. Edmond, barely taller than a bonsai tree, plays the hard-to-please spectator, feigning indifference and yawning noisily. Not those little monkeys again! *Tout le temps, sa même?*—always the same old thing from him? Disconcerted, Ferréol pushes onward to the bush of death's-head weasel's snout. Despite all its little skulls shaking and knocking against each other in the wind, no luck: Edmond remains impassive. He barely holds his nose as they pass the putrid Aristolochia creepers, stinking like rotting meat.

"That's all for today? *Na point in nouveau z'affair? Mette encore, la pas assez!*"—Haven't you got something new? More, more, this isn't enough!

"At your service, master *ti gâté pourri.*"—spoilt-rotten little darling.

No sooner demanded than obtained. Ferréol directs the wheelbarrow towards his very latest acquisition: spider orchids, some yellow, others red-speckled, and lastly, green-streaked. Their delicate long flowers are like giant spider's legs that shake in the wind and all seem to rush at Edmond. It's the first time he's seeing them. One bounces on the edge of the wheelbarrow and then on the child's knee. Terrified, Edmond jumps into the arms of his *ti père*. He screams so much that Ferréol bursts out laughing, and is still chuckling the following day whenever he thinks about it.

Edmond no longer knows whether he's going through a menagerie or a nursery, a garden or paradise.

He gets over his fright, plays at being a wild-animal tamer in front of the giant snapdragons, pesters Grand-Marron to lend him his whip.

That's enough for today!

It's not Grand-Marron who says it, much as he thinks it, but Ferréol, who wants to get back to his catalogues and cuttings of the afternoon, because, in the forests of words, as much as in the forests of Bourbon, he's still searching for an orchid. Not just any orchid. The rarest orchid!

Edmond doesn't know which orchid this is, any more than Ferréol does. He wonders why his master isn't content with the thousands of flowers he already has. This strange habit the Whites have of always wanting more!

Back near the veranda, Edmond points at and names out

loud the crowns-of-thorns, the devil's claws, the firecracker plants, and all the other scarlet species with scary names that the slaves avoid approaching, particularly in November because, they say, around them you can hear the groaning of a cadaver and rattling of a chain that's come straight out of the volcano. Edmond has no time for their two-bit evil spirit Popobawa and his rusty chain. He drinks only Ferréol's words, and a little of the honey syrup that entices him into the storeroom. Edmond questions, Edmond repeats, Edmond learns, since Beaumont says the garden is the best school for him.

By the time Ferréol considers his *ti gâté* to be too old for pushing around in a wheelbarrow, Edmond knows both the common name and the scientific name of every plant, says heliconia when he used to say yellow-tip lobster claw, agapanthus rather than blue ball, *Myosotis sylvatica* as well as forget-me-not. He sometimes says mouse-ear chickweed, sometimes *Cerastium tomentosum*; *Adonis aestivalis* rather than pheasant's eye; *Brassia* when once he'd scream spider orchid. He has enough intelligence—and pollen—for four. *Totoche!*[5] He'd never have believed he'd be adding a load of Latin jargon to his creole patois.

[5] Creole swearword, here expressing amazement and joy.

3
EDMOND DISCOVERS THE GENESIS OF PLANTS
Garden of Eden, golden age

And on the third day, God created plants.

Edmond hasn't opened a single horticultural book, since he doesn't know how to read or write. It's Ferréol who has taught him all you need to know about the world of plants. In fact, once Edmond is five, Ferréol lets him keep a small kitchen garden, which grows with him. At first it just looks like scrub, but Edmond takes such care of it, nose down in the soil, that a few months later, a herb garden and rows of flowers appear. Edmond plants chives, coriander, which he calls *coton-mili*, onions, eggplants, curly parsley, tamarillos. Growing in every corner of his garden are plants that enhance the flavor of the dishes Colombine cooks every day. There's an allspice bush that adds flavors of clove, nutmeg, pepper, and ginger to her cooking, another of kaffir lime, a clove tree, a pimiento plant. Colombine tosses the leaves of these into lamb-and-bean stew, chicken curry, duck casserole, but the pimiento—devil knows why—she adds to anything and everything. Edmond hoes, waters, pours out seeds from sacks bigger than him, eats a few, almost winds up in an early grave. He discovers the meaning of the words toxic, layering, and pollen, and thinks that, all things considered, if he really does have six more lives, in one he'd like to be a bee, a caterpillar, or a branch of verbena.

His love of plants stems from all this, and from the stories that the naturalist Ferréol told him.

Since Edmond was baptized by Father Dalmond, he has officially replaced the Mulungu, the creator deity, of his brother slaves with a certain Jesus, attached to a cross as if to a plant stake, and whom Ferréol considers to be the almighty Father, above Pamphile, above his great-grandfather Martin Joseph. Secretly, Edmond prays as the wind blows, making a soup of his dual culture—Catholic and makondé, creole and *zoreil*.[6] The sky's too big to have just one throne, life too harsh to sweet-talk just one idol.

Ferréol, who knows nothing of Edmond's potpourri of beliefs and fancies, tells him that God—the one who resurrected his mother Mélise and keeps her safe in Heaven—well, that *toubab*[7] created plants on the third day. In winter. Not the fully grown plants, just the seeds and roots. Ferréol tells this story so well that Edmond sometimes gets the impression he made it up himself, but that would be so unseemly, so strange, he instantly banishes the thought from his head. Ferréol says it was so cold that the seeds and roots preferred to stay in the warmth of the soil, like under the big blanket he covers Edmond with from June to September. At the end of winter, they all got together to decide their future. Some of them, the adventurous, bold and reckless, chose to come out of the soil to see close up that famed world of the beyond. The others, more cautious, more sensible, and less curious, preferred to remain under the soil with their friends the earthworms. Fearing they might get mixed up, the seeds and roots kept their original names. Those that went further afield asked to be called stems. God soon noticed that the stems each had their own personality. Some were self-sufficient, ambitious, keen to grow straight up on their own; others showed willingness, application, but were rather spindly; and others were lazy, lying on the ground all day, not shooting up, or barely. Another category was a bit loopy, all floppy, so

[6] Term used to designate a White person who has come from metropolitan France or another European country.

[7] Central and West African name for a White person.

overfamiliar and advantage-taking that it preferred to be permanently supported by another plant. So, there were stems that stood erect, stems that kept shooting upwards, stems that crawled along the ground, known as procumbent, and stems that climbed, which, informally, God called creepers.

The stems and the creepers were so happy to be alive that they kept branching out.

One plant could thus have several stems or hundreds of creepers.

But God felt there was still something missing, that all this was rather austere and the plants looked a bit naked. God thought about it for a long time and, towards the end of spring, he had the idea of making them wear clothes. The news riled the other species—humans, animals, fish, birds—because they each wanted to keep their own sartorial style. So as not to offend any of them, God ruled out hair, feathers, scales, fur, wool, and, of course, fabric. That left only leaves. God hastily invented them. To cover the stems and branches, he created an infinite number of leaves: simple, compound, long, narrow, oval, pointed, split, wavy, serrated, unifoliate, trifoliate, prickly, incised, deciduous, evergreen. God came up with so many types, it almost drove him crazy. Since the humans had kept belts, ties and straps for themselves, God sought a solution to retain the leaves and join them to the stems; after a lot of thought, he added a little tail, slender but strong, which he named a petiole, to the base of the leaves. The petiole linked the leaf directly to the stem, and God would occasionally use one as a toothpick. There were thus seeds, roots, stems, leaves, but God felt that it all still lacked gaiety. So, at the height of summer, he summoned all his angels, who soon came up with something. Upon their advice, he made flowers of every color, every shape, every scent. Next, God read a petition signed by the representative of the bees, butterflies, ants, wasps, flies, ladybugs, and other coleopterous insects, demanding that, in accordance with the right of insects to feed themselves, all flowers in all lands be put at their disposal in all seasons and at every moment of the day. God grumbled but said that was fine. So that there would be blossoms all year round, God arranged for the plants not to flower at the same time. Most refused and confined themselves to summer, but other more conciliatory plants accepted to bloom during the other seasons. And so there were flowers, too, in autumn, winter, and spring. The plants fed on water, light, and soil.

All was going well for the plants and insects until the men and the animals began to suffer from indigestion, due to eating stone soup. The guild of catering trades was consulted, and it suggested that variety be brought to meals. So God added fruits to certain plants, and he himself found them very tasty. The men would eat fruit, especially apples and pears, but before long they were asking for bacon. To avoid offending God, they kept back a few oranges as a gift for the children at Christmas.

As his big celebration drew near, however, God saw that the men were getting bored, and that, in December, they were all falling seriously ill. So God added certain properties to the plants. Some would cure coughs, flu, and fevers, others would make people laugh, dance, and even see God himself, although he preferred to remain anonymous. This time, God had covered everything. He did his annual appraisal and saw that it was good.

But the Devil, jealous, spiteful and sly as ever, visited this vast garden of plants and wanted to sow some mischief. He introduced poisonous plants, hive-causing plants, cacti, and, of course, stinging nettles.

To avoid worsening the situation, God made as if he'd seen nothing.

Across the entire surface of the Earth, there were plants of all kinds—thyme, sunflowers, mint, bay, rosebushes, lily of the valley, ferns, datura, moss, bougainvillea, philodendron, tulips, brambles, dandelions. There were so many plants in so many countries, at so many times of the year, with so many virtues, of so many sizes, shapes, and colors, that God could no longer record them all on his own. He decided to find some men of goodwill, but serious all the same, with a scientific mind, keen on mathematics, to study, enumerate, describe and classify these millions of plants. And that's how he created a new branch of learning: botany. A few fellows—there are always some—did apply to be botanists but were overzealous. Carl von Linné, known also as Carlo Linnaeus, was one of the first volunteers to help God in whom he had great faith. He identified, single-handedly, eight thousand different plants. To avoid the plants being known by a different name from one country to another, Linnaeus gave each one a Latin surname and forename, because in the four corners of the world, from Japan to Timbuktu, Havana to Le Havre, if there was any language that everyone knew, it was Latin. The other botanists—the Jussieu brothers, Philibert Commerson, Jean-Baptiste Bory de Saint-Vincent—don't have the effect on Edmond that Linnaeus does, even though some have roamed his island.

Bory de Saint-Vincent explored Bourbon right up to the Piton de la Fournaise volcano. Ferréol even claims to have met him at the age of nine. Supposedly, the volcanic rock in pride of place on his chest of drawers was given to him by Bory de Saint-Vincent. Edmond wonders whether the vanilla plant Ferréol talks about so often—*Vanilla planifolia*, as his hero Linnaeus would call it—wasn't first mentioned to him by Saint-Vincent. Anyway, one thing is certain, since God is offering work, Edmond is applying to be a botanist.

4

EDMOND, BOTANIST AND DISSIDENT
Ferréol's drawing room, a stormy evening

A botanist, like you!

Edmond is seven when he tells Ferréol that he wants to be a botanist. A botanist because Ferréol is one, a botanist to help him find the rarest orchid in the world, a botanist because his parents live in a kingdom of flowers.

Botany, tree nurseries, greenhouse cultivation, of course his ancestors in Africa would have left all that to the little women. From endlessly eavesdropping behind doors, Edmond has an entirely colonial image of this other place. That of a land all in one piece, from the Sahara to the Cape, roamed by rhinoceros and heavily armed warriors who, between massacres, dine on the grilled flesh and roasted penises of their enemies. When he adds to that the circumcisions done with a machete, the raw scarifications, the evening orgies, and the unions between relatives, Edmond thanks the great *toubab* for having removed him from that load of savagery, and having allowed the Whites to teach him what civilization is.

Back in Africa, they were crazy about the *moringué*, barefisted fighting with kicking, kneeing, and sometimes a stick allowed. Edmond imagines his ancestors, loincloth around hips and amulets around neck, crossing entire regions with a spear, three large knives, a few arrows, their bodies covered in intricate incisions and spectacular tattoos, with slivers of wood inserted under the skin. All that for waging war. The ivory trade, the endless hunts with their tales of panthers, of virgins who no longer are, of gold shortages, that's undoubtedly what would fill their days of truce, facing the Mozambique Channel. A dahlia pinned to the buttonhole of a jacket? What's a jacket? What's a buttonhole? What's a botanist for? What game does a horticulturalist hunt for? Edmond ponders over it; never would they admit to their descendant being a planter of eggplants, *bringelles* in their language, and hibiscus! So Edmond has doubts, hesitates. He imagines their ghosts hurling themselves from Monte Binga while screaming in despair: Edmond, shame on you!

Edmond also knows that *la chance ti poule lé pas la chance ti canard*,[8] that his ancestors are six foot under, between roots and seeds born to sprout. Of course, he'd end up the same, bones and all, he'd return to that compost crawling with worms. But he senses he has a way out, an escape route with this eccentric Ferréol. One evening, after a big dinner attended by Elvire, a few godchildren, and some second cousins, he lingers, heart pounding, in the drawing room, where Ferréol is reading a scathing article in *La Gazette* on a certain Alexandre Dumas, who, not content with being a prolific Parisian author, has the cheek to be Black.

"*Ti père*, it's decided! I'll be a botanist like you and Linnaeus."

Outside, the wind drops, the sky ditches its clouds, a cricket can be heard piercing the twilight calm. Ferréol sits up, rubs his temples. Well, his hearing is really becoming a problem, for a moment he thought Edmond wanted to be a botanist.

"Could you say that again, my dear Edmond? I didn't quite hear."

"I want to be a botanist, like you!"

The cricket stops chirping, Elvire stops knitting, Grand-Marron stops pulling the ear of the dog, who, sensing a bone of contention—not the kind of bone he'd like—thinks he'd best lie down, cross his front paws, and listen to the rumbling thunder.

Ferréol folds his newspaper and lays it on his knees, as he

---

[8] Common Creole proverb, meaning one person's luck isn't another's (literally, the chicken's luck isn't the duck's luck.)

always does when some matter is bothering him. Over there, Dumas is stirring up all of Paris by boasting about writing, and now here, in Bourbon, under his own roof! Could it be a joke?

"What do you mean, Edmond?"

"I want to be a Black botanist."

This takes Ferréol's breath away. He's all emotional, as can be seen from the little drop escaping from his eyes, which are as watery as the mint infusion growing cold on the table. He should have expected it, after talking so much to Edmond about botany, orchids, and greenhouse cultivation. Suddenly, he comes to his senses, like after a stinging slap in the face. Ferréol rubs his cheek and reflects. Did his grandfather put three months of sailing between himself and the Burgundian meadows just for a slave to claim to be the equal of his grandson?

Over there, the peasants would say yes to everything, to the bowl with its quivering dregs of soup; to the endless cycle of paying dues-gruel-sickle-unpaid labor; to the massive feeling of being miniscule. But here, the colonists intended to take their revenge. Indeed, that's how, near enough, the Minister of the Colonies would sell this exile:

SEEKING THE REJECTED OF ALL ORIGINS

TO SWELL THE RANKS OF

THE RÉUNIONNAISE BOURGEOISIE

IN EXCHANGE FOR A PLOT OF STONY GROUND,

WITH NO CERTAINTY OF RETURN,

OR GUARANTEE OF HAPPINESS.

POST-SCRIPTUM: ALL THE COFFEE AND CANE SUGAR YOU LIKE.

Dreaming of a better world, thousands of colonists had embarked and found themselves in Bourbon, uncomfortable, caught with their asses between two Cirques.[9] That of the propertied upper middle class on the one hand, offshoots of an Atlantic or Dauphinoise aristocracy. And that of the multitasking slaves, existential planters-laborers-sloggers on the other. Between the two were the Petits Blancs—or Small Whites. A generic term for an embarrassing swamp of poverty and freedom, of work without prosperity but with resignation, chicken farming, a Sisyphean existence up in Les Hauts, closer to the fog than to the sea. They had to make their slaves work harder than is imaginable, grab the best land available, fall into debt getting there. "There" being the ranks of the middle-class, forever looking over their shoulder, forever with a finger on the trigger to guard against the crazed lunge of a vengeful Negro. In short, they haven't made all these sacrifices—no longer belching at table, giving their little ones private tutors, overcoming all the agricultural crises, investing in factories and a series of arranged marriages, a pair of boots with tassels and thirty-odd Negroes—for one of those Negroes to want to be a botanist or a major landowner like them, on the pretext that his ancestors would have suffered, too. No, no, that definitely cannot happen. They hadn't gone to the trouble of installing these great boundaries of laws, codes, rules of etiquette, these endless barricades, of invisible barbed wire between each clan, rich and poor; each color, Black and white; each category, Gros Blancs and Petits Blancs; of drawing a vertical line between races and colors, reinforced by articles and customs, for an Edmond, from the dizzy heights of his seven years, to want to climb higher than his ass and become a botanist. As if, in life, it was enough to want something to obtain it! What would these *bois-brûlés*, these half-breeds, be demanding tomorrow: liberty, equality?

[9] The three Cirques in La Réunion—Mafate, Salazie and Cilaos—are natural amphitheaters surrounded by verdant crags, which became places of refuge for runaway slaves.

No, no, it really cannot happen. In a corner of the room, busy embroidering a handkerchief, Colombine thinks: he lives in this house, that's already good.

Ferréol is too averse to making long philosophical speeches to explain to Edmond that it's the law of the smartest here, not the right of the weakest. And doesn't he himself risk banishment for bringing up a Cafre child? Does Edmond really have to put him through the mill again? Does he not swallow enough abuse daily because they all, mulattos, Blacks, Whites—Elvire and a few friends excepted—reproach him for pushing a monkey around in a wheelbarrow?

He opts for a way out that's less matter-of-fact, more diplomatic and pragmatic.

"Seven future botanists in the neighborhood, that's far too many. Six is quite enough. You'll be a gardener."

Around him, cousins and godchildren look away, lower their eyes.

"Don't you think?"

Silence of a church.

"Speak up! You all want to be botanists, florists, failing that geologists, don't you?"

Silence of a cemetery.

"Agronomists? Naturalists?"

Silence of the crypt. Ferréol feels a block of ice melting in the center of his chest.

"Apothecaries? Horticulturalists? Nurserymen?"

Silence of a paupers' grave.

"No one! You dare to kill me this way!"

His arms fall, covering the floor with a puddle of pollen.

"What the devil could you do later if it isn't being a botanist?"

Pushed by the others, who know she's sassy, Rose steps forward, rubs her stomach with both hands, and answers: have two children! Her soul-sister Lilas, who never leaves her side, follows suit and shouts: baker! Hévéa, who is kissing her little rosary, murmurs: nun; Ambroise: doctor. Because their mother, on her deathbed, saw a doctor followed by a priest, and went on to live another ten years. Hyacinthe growls: slave hunter, and sticks her tongue out at Edmond. Jasmin pleads for the Bar. Ferréol grits his teeth and purses his lips. Elvire, wishing she'd never been born, offers, for the first time in her life, to take the dog out, while her brother shakes his fists above six heads that, to him, seem hopelessly empty.

Ferréol is tearing his hair out, sparse and white as it's been since his marriage. Elvire, who has followed everything through the window, with the little dog in her arms, makes the sign of the cross. And Ferréol, in a frightful rage, sends everyone out for a breath of air. Why exactly, under his very roof, does no one apart from Edmond want to do the finest job in the world? He can hardly see himself chivvying the director of the Collège de Bourbon, or negotiating ninety francs for boarding school, so that a Cafre can learn to read.

"What of Edmond, then?" Grand-Marron asks, gloating.

Well, Edmond will remain at the house and become a gardener.

Edmond, who intends neither to disobey Ferréol, nor to betray his promise, silently vows, with the Moon watching him from the door and Hyacinth from the window, to be the first black botanist in this Gros-Blancs world, all the same. Botanist and finder of rare flowers.

"Botanist or nothing!" he screams, before running out of the room.

5
FERRÉOL BELLIER-BEAUMONT
Bellevue neighborhood, end of the 18th century

His first drawing was of a rose framed with pumpkins, a total horror painted directly on the curtain. Onto this drawing, which everyone still thought splendid, he grafted a certainty and a pledge: he would become a botanist.

otanist or nothing!"
It is with these that, from the age of three, Ferréol opens his eyes, which are the green of the bougainvillea in his garden. Before sitting at the table for some *riz chauffé*, or warmed-up rice, Ferréol already has his hands full of yellowing petals, dried-up branches, or gray-ringed caterpillars, which he runs to place on a pile of dead leaves. Some people have blood on their hands, Ferréol has pollen on his fingertips.

He was born in the island of Bourbon on a Saturday, June 2, 1792, between a brother and two sisters who had the same parents but not the same destiny. And between his brothers and sisters yet to be born, and the family members at death's door, he grows up like Edmond, surrounded by rag dolls and bunches of chrysanthemums. Despite the thirty-seven-year gap between them, the differences diminish, the resemblances multiply. At four, Ferréol gambols along the fragrant paths of the garden, around the agapanthus, anthurium and ferns. Edmond does, too. At six, they both say prayers at the sight of a dead leaf, and faint in front of a forest fire. Other kids can hunt for treasure, have saber fights with one-eyed pirates, or track down fugitive slaves in remote Cirques. Ferréol and Edmond prefer the watering can and pruning knife to toy daggers and pistols!

At fourteen and a day, Ferréol knows the Latin name of all the plants of the Côte-au-Vent. At seven years and five days, Edmond knows the Greek root of the trees' names, the Roman etymology of the flowers, and a whole load of other things that his *ti père* is happy to pass on to him. At sixteen and a bit, Ferréol talks to the lilies, claims they understand, feels his heart flutter for the first time reading Boyceau's *Traité du jardinage selon les raisons de la nature et de l'art*, a thing of eighty-seven pages, with drawings of parterres and planting techniques, that Elvire gave him for his birthday. At eight-and-a-half, Edmond is a Ferréol without a moustache who buries forever the cheerful world of childhood for the solemn and serious demeanor of the model pupil. From the age of seventeen, Ferréol is studying at the Collège de Bourbon; at the same age, Edmond has, according to his master, something worth more than science: experience. Knowledge is passed from the mouth of one into the head of the other, who may never know the four operations of arithmetic, but has the memory of an elephant. Edmond makes do with what he has and what people deign to give him.

From the age of eighteen, every Saturday, Ferréol gives Elvire, his favorite sister, a bunch of red Ixora tied with string bitten off with his teeth. From then on, these two are inseparable. As adults, they each live in adjacent properties separated by a hedge of sage—eighty centimeters that both Edmond and the geese jump over with a cackle. They mix in the same circles, with the Patu de Rosemont brothers, the Lepervanches, a lower middle class with big ideas, dreaming one moment of a train, the next of a metal bridge, and then of a free press for this island where everything needs doing.

One afternoon when they are all together, Ferréol is celebrating his twentieth birthday. Before a bed of orchids and some enthusiastic friends, he stands up and declares that he will be a grower rising to a botanist.

"Is that all?" someone asks.

"It's quite enough!" he replies.

The land belongs to all those who work it, flowers to those

who look at them. He will build himself up on his own in an island yet to be built, and walk around with a bag loaded with labels and secateurs, busy recording all the plants. With him he'll have three coarse-linen smocks, a few gardening tools, and a single language, that of flowers.

Reckoning that he's spoken enough, for eighteen months no one hears his voice anymore! Over the following years, Ferréol covers the island of Bourbon from top to bottom, joins expeditions towards the volcano, jots down in notebooks the names of plants, specimens of which he stores in cloth bags or herbariums. On certain mornings, Elvire, still in bed, hears the sound of a pickax disemboweling the earth outdoors. Ferréol is back, plants some seeds, stocks up on biscuits and dried meat, before setting off again to no one knows where to look for other seeds to be used for no one understands what. In this way, he spends entire weeks, months, half-years on voyages of discovery.

Returning from an expedition, Ferréol walks past the hut of a freed slave whom his own slaves call "the healer." He's an old Cafre of seventy-five who thinks that everything, including hemorrhoids, malaria, fever and cholera, can be healed with decoctions and infusions of creepers from the forest. As a last resort, when dying, even the most rational colonists come to consult him. Never in daylight. They set off under cover of star-studded darkness, horrified at the thought of being recognized by some insomniac passerby. Squinting, they walk on tiptoe with a sack of rice on their shoulders and beside them, a live sheep with hooves padded and muzzle tied shut. The healer barely hears the muffled sound of the half-dozen feet and hooves that stop dead outside his door. Behind it lies a massive labyrinth of creepers: flame vine, devil's ivy, *liane savon*, zigzag, key liana, allamanda, turpeth bindweed, basket vine, jade climber, butterfly pea, balloon vine, devil's backbone. Creepers galore, snaking over the partitions, from top to bottom, right to left, hanging like garlands from the ceiling, creating an olive-hued tapestry on the walls, a green tide on the floor. And thus, one morning, standing before this tangle of creepers running right up to the door, there's Ferréol, or rather, a mouth agape under eyes like saucers. He's twenty-eight years old. Never seen so many creepers in all his life! A voice from the back of the hut invites him in. Ferréol declines the offer, claims he's just passing by, just wants to take a look.

"*Moin lé in guérisseur, pas in musée*"—I'm a healer, not a museum—says the old Cafre.

"I'm a botanist, not sick," Ferréol replies.

"There's no one sicker than a healthy man," says the healer, indicating a chair.

Ferréol hesitates, enters reluctantly, barely sits on the edge of the solitary chair. He drinks, almost regretfully, the rubber-vine beverage that's poured out for him. But the more he drinks, the more Ferréol relaxes. To the healer, who says nothing, Ferréol at first speaks little, then more, then a lot, and finally, too much. In an uninterrupted monologue lasting two hours and twenty-five minutes, his whole truth pours out, like rum escaping from an overturned barrel: his love of plants, his vocation to be a botanist, his negligible discoveries, the dream of an encyclopedia of some three hundred pages, to which he'd give the title, *Liber florum et herbarum exoticarum*.

"Leave this book stuff to the termites. You've got it wrong!" the old Cafre objects. "Since you were four, you've been looking for treasure you'll find in no book. What you're looking for will be both right under your nose and hard to find. You're looking for the rarest orchid on Earth."

Ferréol smiles, maybe blushes. His silence lasts what seems like a century, while he's wondering to what extent this healer is mad. So, he's searching for the rarest orchid in the world, is he? When he could have thousands of flowers? He'd have to visit it, that world, when his is limited to Bourbon. Ferréol serves himself some more of that hot vine infusion, its curls of steam drawing a petal in the evening air. As he drinks, he ponders and mutters to himself. What's the point of looking for the rarest orchid? Why?

Through the din of his silent thoughts and questions, Ferréol nevertheless senses this "why" turning into why not, why ever not, and, finally, into how and where to find this orchid that's so rare. Ferréol is twenty-eight years and twenty-eight days old. Half of his life is, he believes, behind him. The second half remains to be written. He has neither wife nor child, none of the ball-and-chains his friends have clamped to their feet after short-lived nuptials. He can come and go as he pleases, hunt for a flower, bunches of them even. If he doesn't find the rarest orchid in the world, he thinks, he'll at least pick the rarest on the island of Bourbon.

Suddenly feeling crazily elated, Ferréol closes the healer's door and plunges into the cool of the night, with a lantern in his right hand that barely lights up his toes.

And that's how the obsession with orchids came to him.

The months go by, the years, too. The island of Bourbon gets covered in mills, worked by steam, animals, arms; and in roads to enlarge the tracks; and in sugarcane plantations to replace the coffee ones. As for Ferréol, he's covered in shame. At thirty, he doesn't think he's found any plant exceptional enough to make him a botanist worthy of the name. He's spent the past two years hoping, imagining himself to be more than he is. Like a builder kids himself that he's an architect, a groom that he's an equestrian.

"Having a greenhouse, dozens of notebooks, boxes of seeds, never turned anyone into a botanist," he laments to himself.

He certainly owns some unusual species—a cactus in the form of a brain; nipple fruit; three mandrakes; white strawberries with red achenes; a few carnivorous plants; a bed of star-like edelweiss that give a Swiss touch to his tropical garden. Ferréol even has a white egret orchid, which is so much more beautiful than anything else he's found that he believes, for a time, that this marvel in the form of a white bird with outspread wings is the rare flower he seeks. Until the day a botanist back from Asia tells him that it grows like brambles absolutely everywhere east of the Volga, including in the kingdom of Siam, China, Japan, and even on the edge of the ruined wells of Korea. Ferréol can't accept this and his vexation causes him to lose weight. For four months almost entirely spent sitting on a chair, its back now thicker than he is, he's devastated at being, at best, just an unmarried grower of saffron, at worst a planter of watercress, rosemary, and lemongrass.

Elvire sobs, Colombine is panic-stricken, all the more since, one New Year's day, their troubling botanist makes the strange vow never to raise his eyes to Heaven again unless he has been sent a sign on Earth. From now on, Ferréol walks with head down, and dines with forehead low, chin stuck to stomach. Grand-Marron asks for him, he doesn't lift his head up. He no longer sees the summit of the mountains. No longer watches the white-tailed tropicbirds beneath the white clouds. His gaze remains somewhere around the level of the daisies. His personal strength and his hope will come from the earth, or not at all.

At thirty-one years, six months and fifteen days old, Ferréol, a bachelor on an island with a ratio of one woman to four men, is nevertheless obliged to look up, one early afternoon, when Angélique Dejean lifts his chin and stares deep into his eyes. With cheeks covered in tears, and black dress covered with a dark shawl, the adolescent—fifteen, maybe sixteen years old—weeps timidly while asking him for some gardenias, mauve pansies, a few small branches, to adorn two coffins. Surprised to see the hem of a bell-shaped skirt other than Elvire's, Ferréol, his forehead beaded with sweat, spits on the floor and grumbles to himself.

Between Angélique and him, it began the way it would end, with grunting and pain in front of a bed of cemetery plants. Everything about their meeting seemed to augur a future pierced with sorrow, but blinded as they were by that two-o'clock sun, distorting their vision and reason, they believed in everything, including the worst.

6
MONSIEUR ET MADAME DEJEAN
Quartier-Français, 1823

Monsieur and Madame Dejean died on the same day,
but not of the same thing.

Edmond has never seen a portrait of Angélique, or an item of her clothing. Out of politeness more than kindness, he places a bouquet of blue hydrangeas on her grave when Ferréol, gripping his hand tight, pays his respects there every November 1. The pickax Blacks, who labor at jobs of every description, drop like flies all around him and no one makes a big fuss about that. Edward concludes that death is part of life, and gets used to stories of couples that end badly.

It was the man in charge of the henhouse who told him Angélique's story. And what stories he had to tell, too! Before being appointed manager of the yard, he was a dry, dull and silent man, whose wife gave birth to a premature baby so small he could be held in the palm of a hand. They gave him one day to live, two at most. During that time his father prayed, calling for help from all the gods of the Earth. After a week, the baby opened his eyes but remained dumb, as if being snatched from the dead had been so traumatic that he'd lost his voice. This wordless child did, however, have such sharp hearing that he could pick up the sliding of snails on the back of leaves and the murmuring of the river a league further down. This acute hearing meant that he loved stories, those made up so you have sweet dreams in your bed, those written to make you want to leap out of it at first light. So his father began telling and telling and telling countless stories, sad or preposterous, true or unreal, funny or even fantastical, with red dragons, will-o'-the-wisps, pirates' treasure. The child is entranced, laughs, cries.

You can see it in his eyes and the way his lips move. Edmond isn't allowed to join in because Ferréol forbids him from listening to this far-fetched balderdash from a born fantasist, but one evening he does get to hear the father telling the boy his legend of the Dejeans.

February 15, 1823. On the heights of Sainte-Suzanne, near a waterfall, Monsieur Dejean was killed by a bird, probably a *papangue*, the island's only bird of prey, that dropped a tortoise onto his bald head, easily mistaken for a stone. The shell shattered, as did Monsieur Dejean's skull. While the raptor was picking, indiscriminately, at the flesh of the one and the brain of the other, a servant passing by recognized Monsieur Dejean's differently colored eyes. Once he'd put the pieces of his skull back together, he slid a mirror between his teeth. Since there was no condensation, he concluded that Monsieur Dejean wasn't pretending, and ran to break the cruel news to the family.

Madame Dejean choked to death on the slice of pineapple in her mouth when she was told the news. Of the two of them, only three mementos remained: the bloodstain on the rocks of the Délices waterfall; a pineapple crown that remained on the veranda table for ten years; and a young girl no one had ever seen: Angélique. Her parents had shut her away in a Christian school, where the Lasallians taught reading, arithmetic, needlework, silence, and solemnity. She was sent for, a brief wake was organized. The police contacted the notary, who arrived with an assistant.

To their only daughter, then seventeen, the Dejeans left twenty slaves, nine pigs, a horse, forty-eight kilos of silverware, and an acre of land in Sainte-Suzanne. Once the inventory of the estate had been made, the remains of the two parents were buried in good worm-rich soil, and a guardian was sought for Angélique. To everyone's surprise, no one volunteered. Angélique didn't get a guardian but did find a fiancé, which, according to the neighbors, was far better. A month later, the banns were published.

On April 1, 1823, under a jacaranda-blue sky, in the middle of a garden where the bees were dancing, Pierre Ferréol Edmé Bellier-Beaumont married Marie-Périne Antoinette Angélique Dejean, with Elvire handing them the wedding rings. Secretly, deep down, Ferréol thinks: what if she is that rare plant he's searching for?

For the first six months of the marriage, Angélique swooned over her husband who spoke to begonias and was up at dawn to hand-pollinate watermelons and squashes. After nine months, she was heaving at the sight of this man who, like all the rest, would blow his nose by pressing a nostril with one finger, and clear his throat with all the grating of a pulley. Ferréol's nocturnal snoring, which sounded like a valve and rumbled like a drum, echoed through the house. After one year, Angélique decided to sleep sitting up, her back wedged between cushions. After two, she changed bedroom, after two-and-a-half, she changed building. She finally settled for good in the west wing of their house in Sainte-Suzanne. They had no children, thus lopping off all branches of their family tree.

Ferréol, who still loved kids, would treat any he came across to blossom honey and Surinam cherries, whether godchildren, first cousins, or neighbors' offspring. Rose, Lila, Hévéa, Hyacinthe, Ambroise, and Jasmin were among them.

With the passing of years and the damp sky of the eastern towns, everything inside the house, and their couple, had taken on water: the first hesitant, uncertain drops of rain had initially warped the back of the still-life tapestry, turning, here and there, into timid rivulets trickling down the walls. Then, from the roof, marble-sized drops started to fall in boldly vertical lines; these new drops filled the earthenware pitcher that a slave had placed there just in time. Very soon, other drops had turned up, confident and proud, that were caught in cast-iron basins and wine ewers. And still others, more reckless, started bouncing on the table and turning half the parquet into a giant puddle, and all on a Sunday, while everyone was dozing at Mass. Finally, ten other leaks, barely a few meters apart, started whipping the shoulders of the slaves, who, shielding foreheads with hands, placed containers everywhere, before the masters got back from the sermon.

For six months of the year, the Dejean-Beaumont couple would undertake large-scale insulation work and caulk the gilded paneling of their ceiling. For the other six months, they would observe the bitter failure of the enterprise. They had no other choice but to live with the incessant plip-plopping, between stormy sky and floorcloths; they would dine in their drawing room under little whalebone umbrellas, which they held with their right hand while the left fumbled in the soggy bread basket that Colombine, in rubber boots and hooded cape, held out to them. The servants, who had grown up under this roof of rain and lightning, would organize obstacle races between the puddles and the carafes, and, much to their master's annoyance, never chase away the little snails and slugs making merry under the four-poster bed. Ferréol got fungal infections on his damp feet. Angélique wept tears that mingled with the rainwater Grand-Marron would bail out all day long.

She fell sick. Fever, perhaps; exasperation, certainly.

On April 9, 1827, Angélique died after four years of a marriage that was hard to digest in every respect. She was twenty years old.

Ferréol lived alone, weighed down by apathetic slaves who just roamed around the cane fields and orchards. Their breathing, their gait, their figures—everything irritated him by reminding him of the woman who had abandoned them at the start of an austral winter that would never end. More than his widowerhood, he was upset at not having found the rare orchid that still eluded him.

From then on, Ferréol occupied one wing of the house, and Elvire lived in the other. Colombine served as a mailman sans mailbag between the two. Like all unhappy people at that time, Ferréol was tempted by cane wine and acrimony. He opted for sleeps lasting several days, from which he emerged with thoughts of rope and hanging.

Elvire, now an old maid of thirty-seven, feared seeing her brother die. She replaced their mother, even in her way of dressing and styling her hair, called Ferréol "my child, my little one," and never took her eyes off him. Every rose has its thorn: Ferréol could no longer do without his sister, Elvire didn't have the time to marry.

After Angélique's death, all Ferréol had left was botany, the impartiality of orchids and long, solitary walks. Two years passed by like two centuries, long and oppressive, until the morning when, in a neighboring barn, a slave gave birth to her only son: Edmond. And that's where the man in charge of the henhouse had ended his evening story, because, turning his head to the door, he had seen Edmond, quietly listening.

7
EDMOND AS SEEN BY VOLCY-FOCARD
Memories and *Notice*, 1830-1840

*Later, when they would be plagued with aches and pains,
smelling of old age and the earth itself, they would still
remember him as an intelligent child.*

Since declaring out loud that he wants to be a botanist, Edmond is never more than a bush away from his *ti père*. Sometimes hot on his heels, forever his shadow. As promised, Ferréol makes him his gardener. He also gives Edmond a pencil and a notebook with some unused pages. Edmond covers them with scribbles he calls words or drawings. He only knows how to write his name, nothing else, but to make up for all shameful ignorance, he retains fast, retains by heart, all that he hears, breathes, sees. The story and characteristics of each orchid, Ferréol's way of handling them, the scent of the blooms, the faces of the botanists sketched in the journals. Same gait, same facial expression, Edmond soon becomes the echo of his master, a reflection in the mirror of his eyes. He walks around like him, thumbs tucked into the armholes of his waistcoat, knows almost all that his master does about flora, to such an extent that he soon knows more plant names, more species of orchid, than he does the names of the hired workers, the freed slaves and the actual slaves who work, or used to work, on the estate. Ferréol's friends confirm this. Among them, Eugène Volcy-Focard, clerk of the court and amateur naturalist. Every Sunday, Elvire's veranda turns into a merry table of notaries, attorneys, and merchants whose birth and occupation serve as their invitation card. Volcy-Focard, a portly public official who smells of eau de Cologne and the wood-paneling of courtrooms, is invited, on January 4, 1841, to the first such gathering of the year. After dessert, Ferréol no longer fancies giving a tour of his nursery, as planned. Edmond replaces him, showing Volcy-Focard around. The clusters of red flowers on the two royal poinciana trees guarding the entrance to the house trumpet that summer is at its height in Bourbon. Inside Ferréol's nursery, Volcy-Focard follows Edmond closely. Between anecdotes about Ferréol's latest acquisition—a teak tree from Arabia, which Edmond points out using its Latin name, *Tectona grandis*—Edmond moves from flower to flower with the lightness of a butterfly. He speaks of *Hedychium gardnerianum*. He extols all the virtues of *Alpinia purpurata*, ideal for a cough and sore throat. Before Volcy-Focard, he qualifies the danger of *Datura stramonium*: more hallucinogenic than poisonous. He's amazed that the large creamy-white flowers of the *Beaumontia grandiflora* are already out.

"*Par Mulungu! Na pu de saison.*"—By Mulungu! There are no more seasons.

The walk lasts three hours, during which forty-nine orchids, fifty-one other flowering plants, and twenty-seven species of tree are shown, named, described in great detail, from top to roots. By the end, Volcy-Focard's head is a whirl of words, colors, descriptions, and smells, sending it spinning so fast, he holds it in his hands as if it were about to explode. Edmond pulls him gently by the arm and makes him sit down on the aerial roots of a giant filao with its filiform leaves. He brings over a few *Cannabis sativa* leaves for the court clerk to chew, while still listing for him all the other known species of hemp.

"*Voilà in bon remède, goute ta war!*"—A fine remedy, he says, try it, you'll see!

Volcy-Focard is impressed by the knowledge of this young Cafre naturalist of barely twelve years old. Twenty years later, according to what we read in his *Notice sur l'introduction et la fécondation du vanillier a l'île Bourbon*, he's still lauding his talent to all his friends, telling them of an illiterate African botanist who speaks only Creole but names plants using the scientific jargon of Linnaeus and Jussieu. Edmond remains proud of, and pleased with, this testimony all his life.

Edmond considers himself fortunate because he wasn't thrown alive into the Grande Rivière Saint-Jean at birth. A slave under the age of eight, nine, is like a drunkard who drinks, eats, sleeps. Neither useful, nor profitable, nor sellable. But Edmond has neither the face of an old man, nor the deformed fingers from tying up bundles of wood for ten hours a day. As for the rising at five, the sun searing the skin, he's only really familiar with them when he's in his personal kitchen garden, which now measures ninety square meters. He moans a bit when Ferréol orders him to pull up the weeds, grumbles when the estate has to be cleaned, but thanks his lucky stars that he's a gardener. He even thinks he's too spoilt. He spends his late afternoons sorting the *brèdes*, or leaves, of chayotes, pumpkins, *mafane*, or para cress, pak choy, nightshade, sow thistle, moringa—spinach-like greens that Colombine cooks with ginger, garlic, salt, and Ferréol requests every day. When the others are breaking their backs in the sugarcane fields, weeping over their arms being crushed to the elbow by the mill, he, Edmond, is dragging around study books, boxes of pencils, portable greenhouses, glass containers packed with seeds. When he falls asleep, head on the table, he dreams that he's a great botanist, discussing the differences between night-blooming jasmine and star jasmine with Philibert Commerson: I'm telling you, the flowers of *Cestrum nocturnum* only open at nightfall and their scent is the sweetest, the most potent, of all floral scents. Nothing like the *Trachelospermum jasminoides*, known as star jasmine, which is less scented, more fragile. The pitaya? What about the pitaya? I've already told you. It's also called dragon fruit; it only flowers and can be fertilized at night, from September to December! No, Commerson, you may be a Burgundian, but you're no less of a goddamn fool. Commerson recognizes his faults, literally turns in his grave, and pulls his cover of white lilies up to his ashamed eyes, which stand out on his wild-haired head. He's amazed to be repudiated by an eight-year-old child, secretly admires him. By Jove! The new guard is already there.

When he is neither dreaming nor in the garden, Edmond is the only slave at Bellevue to open a book behind Ferréol's back. He tries to decipher the pages of his manuals and other texts on young shoots, or the circulation of sap. He was flabbergasted when he first understood that all those scribbles to the left had a meaning and formed the words he spoke all day long. He rushed off to explain it to Isidore, a Malagasy boy the same age as him. But Isidore couldn't care less that that jumble is a sentence and each page part of a story. All that interests him is the cassava and mango he chops into big chunks at lunchtime. It's not his fault he's a machine. He's been taught to think little, feel nothing, and consider only what's useful. Cutting cane, threshing beans, corn or wheat, plaiting chayote straw, nothing else. Isidore works, Isidore keeps quiet. He still has three buckets to fill at the river, corn to top. Tomorrow's Sunday, the day for rub-downs and cleaning in the stables at Bellevue. By one o'clock, he'll already be off-duty. So, if he's finished tidying all the gear in the barn, if his back, hunched as a zebu's, isn't aching too much, if this pain hammering the soles of his feet leaves him be, maybe then he'll listen to all the nonsense spouted by that fake, that *canne fraudée* Edmond, on manuals, vanilla plants, the naming of spring onions.

Edmond could pride himself on being superior to the other slaves, because what counts is not being tall, so much as being a head above the rest. No! Until he seizes his destiny and understands why his mother brought him into the world, he wants to know everything, learn everything, try everything, including the artificial and manual pollination of flowers, Ferréol's new occupation.

8
CHARLES MORREN
Belgium, 1837

It started with pumpkins and greenhouse cultivation.

Edmond is eight when, on one March 15, at six in the morning, Ferréol first teaches him how to distinguish between male and female flowers on a pumpkin creeper. Ferréol describes it in a letter from 1862 to Volcy-Focard: "I got him to help me with the pollination of the flowers of a plant of the pumpkin family called 'jolifiat.' In this plant, the male and female flowers are separate and grow on different branches, so I taught the little Black boy, Edmond, to pick the male flowers and place them carefully onto the female ones, which, underneath, carry the embryo of the fruit, as with all pumpkins."

Four weeks earlier, Ferréol sowed pumpkin, squash, zucchini and winter-squash seeds, followed by Edmond, carrying the tools. Edmond began by turning over the soil, digging eight parallel furrows, and laying mulch on the ground. Ferréol launched into an almost military maneuver—"Forward march! Bend over! Three seeds! Stand, march! Bend over . . . "—placing three pumpkin seeds into a hole the size of a ladybug, every meter. With each of them taking a furrow, they advanced like soldiers, serious as if on a field of honor.

A month later, on that March 15, they see that, on the plot, a bed of creeping procumbent stems has emerged, each with four or five leaves and budding flowers.

"On a female flower, Edmond, there's something resembling a little fruit. That's the ovary. Male flowers are shorter and generally flower in clusters. The pollen grains are on the male organs, also called stamen. There are two methods of hand-pollination."

And Ferréol takes up a small splinter of wood, touches the center of the male flower, collects the pollen, places it in contact with the female flower, and tells Edmond to meet him again, right there, in three months' time.

One hundred and ten days after the sowing, Edmond, returning to see the pumpkin creepers, discovers a field of orangey moons, a vegetable garden full of potbellied pumpkins that promise plenty of tarts and veloutés. That year, Ferréol makes the newspapers for having harvested an eighty-kilo pumpkin, so broad and tall that it's hollowed out, left to dry, then varnished, making it a cradle for the twins his neighbors, the Villeroys, have just brought into the world.

That same year, 1837, while they are making a pumpkin tart together, Ferréol informs Edmond that far, far away, in Belgium, a country as flat as a pancake and as damp as the Takamaka valley in Saint-Benoît, a botanist has discovered how to manually pollinate the flower of a very rare orchid, the flower of the vanilla plant, so that it produces fruit. He's called Charles Morren and grows the orchid in a hothouse between a candelabra cactus and that splendid Aztec discovery that's all the rage in Bourbon, tomatoes. Charles Morren's vanilla plant produced fifty-four fruit, fifty-four pods ready to be picked a year after he'd hand-pollinated the flowers. And that's how that little rascal Edmond discovers the story of vanilla, one orchid among the fifty-odd that Ferréol owns, to the left of the house. Until now, he would spot it, but not linger. It's a spice plant that has stems, leaves, flowers, but stubbornly refuses to produce any fruit.

9
HERNÁN CORTÉS
Mexico-Seville, 16th century

Through the forests of the Aztec empire, the baskets overflowing with vanilla would be brought down to the town.

The story of vanilla didn't take root under Belgian arbors or the forests of Bourbon, in the shade at the foot of the cabbage trees, Dracaena, and coconut palms Edmond pees against. It's a farce that comes from much further back, from the 16th century, and from the jungles of Mexico, like the corn flour gruel, the *soso-maïs*, he eats once or twice a week.

Edmond doesn't know where Mexico is, any more than he knows the tropic of his ancestors. He just repeats that, in both cases, everything begins with light-skinned men on the black sand of a deserted beach. But in the story of vanilla, those helmeted men, with fiery eyes and bushy beards, are called *conquistadores*, and their leader is Hernán Cortés. In both stories, it's the same old song. On the port side, pyramids that float on the ocean; foreigners who land with one hand on the heart, the other on the scabbard; on the starboard side, entire villages that can't imagine they'll be taken over by players of castanets, drinkers of sangria, and worse, planters of pomegranates! Edmond knows that it takes but a minute to go from being a free man to a slave. Not a slave of the Whites. That comes much later. But of a little leader just as dark-skinned as you are, usually. As the corollary of his victory in some awful war, or as payment demanded for some debt. As for so many others, the door of freedom then closes forever more. Bang! Double-locked. You are always the victim of the barbarity of your own people before being the victim of the venality of others.

In Mexico, the thudding of boots, the horses stamping . . . Edmond can vividly imagine it as he listens to Ferréol's stories in front of his vanilla plants. He tells of Cortés, and Edmond sees him as a tall, bare-headed devil advancing with his army of flamenco dancers towards a city he believes to be made of gold. To his right, Lake Texcoco. To his left, Doña Marina, alias La Malinche, interpreter, lover, and adviser. Before him, the emperor Montezuma. Above him, words of welcome. Glory to the foreigners. November 9, 1519.

"Montezuma, Cortés!"

"Cortés, Montezuma!"

Naturally, the introductions last ten hours, watched by priests, warriors, and princesses. Edmond imagines himself there, fingers covered in rings, costume in feathers, beside a basket full of offerings, between a majordomo and two ambassadors. To mark the occasion, the emperor's chamberlain serves some *pulque*, which relaxes everyone and makes Montezuma a little tipsy. Cortés, who holds his drink better, and puts business before pleasure, is just rising to give his speech on dialogue between peoples and international trade, when Montezuma murmurs to him that he drinks up to twenty goblets of chocolate with vanilla a day to satisfy his wives and thwart the male menopause. Cortés sits back down. All things considered, business can wait. Montezuma is pleased with himself. Let a tankard of vanilla-flavored chocolate be brought to our guest! He will see what he will see!

And that's how the Spaniards discovered vanilla, its pod wide as a finger and long as two fingers. Apple-green when just picked, chocolate-brown once scalded and dried. An exceptional taste, unforgettable, unique in the world, according to Cortés. A sweet, warm note of caramel and cocoa that reminds him of summer, strolls in the woods along the Guadalquivir river, the languorous kisses of Doña Marina. And that aroma! That almost aphrodisiac aroma, at once animal and spicy. Cortés declares himself conquered by the fruit of this wild orchid, and promises that one day, it will see Seville.

1529. The return journey. Along the floating gardens of his new Spain, Cortés pulls up a few cuttings of vanilla, covered in flowers. Promises are made to be kept. He advances amid hummingbirds, ladybugs, and bees, not suspecting that they are the keepers of a very big secret. It's a bee that pollinates the vanilla. No bee, no fruit. While the Aztecs carry the secret of their sacred plant to their graves, Cortés stamps on a blasted bee that seems intent on halting his progress. Under his arm, a box full of jet-black vanilla pods, a little greasy, at once supple and glossy. In the other hand, vanilla creepers, their leaves still green. He's already smiling at the thought of all the pesos this spice will make him, at the renown that will be attached to his name.

Standing on the deck of the ship, he thinks for one last time of those barbarian Aztecs, so resistant to Christianity. To his second-in-command, who asks him what should be done with the last survivors of that twilight civilization, Cortés—via Edmond, who knows this story by heart—simply replies:

"Slaughter those cut-throats for me! And Seville, here we come."

Seville at that time is a Babel on which flocks of foreigners converge—*pícaros*, or rogues, and vagabonds, drawn by its reputation for wealth and its excellent cigarettes. But mostly, the cohabitation of consulates, bandits, opportunists, misunderstandings, hatreds means that Seville stinks! Right across the city, it smells. Of scheming, plotting, burying. However, as Cortés's ship enters the port, the customs officers from the *Casa de contratación* are flabbergasted. A fabulous aroma of vanilla, heady and sensual, rises from the hold, descends from the rigging, the mast, the sailors' armpits, condenses on the deck and washes over the city, smothering its stew of enduring bad smells.

For thirty-five days, Seville no longer smells of trouble. There's no more scheming, no more fighting with this strange new perfume clinging to your body. All the nostrils of the city, smooth or hairy, broad or narrow, fine or thick, are penetrated by invisible notes of oriental spice, tobacco, and a potent trace of ambergris. On the parade ground, yesterday's enemies greet each other like brothers. In the gutters, cats produce kittens. Escaping from under caravans, behind beer barrels, the bedrooms of plush apartments, are the echoes of kisses, breathless voices, marriage proposals. A whole current of unspeakable tranquility, rabid goodness, excessive tenderness sweeps through Seville wherever the vanilla and its musky aroma pass.

The king comes to observe the phenomenon for himself.

"Who should be thanked?"

"Vanilla!"

"Who is that?"

"His Majesty means *what* is that," comes the obsequious correction.

"An orchid from Mexico brought here by Cortés. Its fruit is the rarest on Earth."

"It's a fragrant pod. It's as valuable as gold!"

This last piece of information convinces the emperor. Charles the Fifth orders that cuttings be planted everywhere, including in his kitchen garden in Belem. While waiting for the vanilla plants to flower, he adopts a kitten, gets his wife pregnant, and drinks cups of tea flavored with vanilla.

Twelve years later, the cat dies of an ulcer, the child claims the throne, the stock of vanilla pods has long been exhausted. Not a single vanilla plant in Spain has borne fruit!

17th century. A box stamped "Kingdom of France—Aztec souvenir" arrives at the Louvre Palace. King Louis hands the box to his master gardener, Jean Le Nôtre, who plants a vanilla cutting in the royal kitchen garden. The vanilla plant flourishes in the Tuileries Garden, climbs right up the elms and the marble statues, threatens the chairs on the Grande Allée, trips up the courtiers. That's enough! It is transplanted to the orangery, where it is politely forgotten.

Spring 1819, thus much later on, the plants have been moved from the Tuileries to Versailles, where the new king, Louis XVIII, resides. When some concern spoils his day, he likes to walk along the paths of the garden, dragging his boots, leaving tracks in the dust. He passes a vanilla plant, asks his personal gardener what it is, what that plant is doing there. It's explained to him. He hesitates between two orders: get the whole bush pulled up, or, as with all troublesome, useless, or dangerous sorts, exile it to Cayenne, or to Bourbon. One creeper more or less in those forests overseas, what difference would it make? He is told that the orchid already grows in the Amazon rainforest. The second destination gets his approval. The gardener receives the order to pack the vanilla-plant stems in a box, which he then places on board one of three caravels setting sail for Bourbon. The first caravel sinks off Senegal. The second is partly destroyed by fire. The third transports the vanilla in its padded wooden chest. Among the crew is the botanist Perrotet, charged with importing the vanilla plant to Bourbon.

There are always botanists on sea voyages, with their portable greenhouses, dry rhizomes, glass boxes stuffed with seeds, and new plants in tow. At sea, they sleep in individual cabins, dine at the captain's table, fill the ship's log with observations on phytoplankton, red algae, sand couch-grass. That particular botanist, Perrotet, received a clear order from the captain, a certain Philibert: to develop some new species on Bourbon, brought back from the Indies or the New World, to rival what those Portuguese raptors and Spanish vultures were up to. He says "brought back" whereas the natives scream "stolen," the end justifying the means.

Once he's arrived at his destination, Perrotet distributes cuttings to various growers from different parishes, and plants a vanilla cutting in Saint-Denis, in the Jardin du Roy, a local replica of the Jardin des Plantes in Paris, but with fewer plants and more lizards than its big brother along the Seine. The vanilla plant has a great old time, attaching itself to all manner of supports. It climbs right up the stakes and wattle fences, scales the filaos, yuccas, Barbados-nut and mango trees. It even clings to the island's very first gas streetlamp, positioned at the entrance to the Jardin du Roy. The vanilla plant flourishes everywhere, forming a tangle of creepers so thick, so dense, with leaves so fleshy, broad and abundant, that any support could no longer be seen. But, stubborn and true to form, the plant produces not a single vanilla pod. Perrotet sets sail again, heading for the Philippines. In his absence, he entrusts the vanilla cultivation to an assistant gardener, who waits, waits, and waits some more. His hermit-like patience sees ten months go by, two years, finally three, the passing time measured by the beard slowly growing down to his navel. 1822. The assistant gardener dies, the botanist Marchand takes over; he reintroduces a few more cuttings to the island of Bourbon. All the vanilla plants grow taller, their flowers open, but still no fruit. Edmond exclaims, angrily:

"All that for just that!"

In 1833, thus eleven years later, the governor, Jacques Philippe Cuvillier, wants to revive vanilla cultivation on Bourbon. During a lengthy tour, punctuated by endless talks, he stops at Sainte-Suzanne. He sets out the risks of monoculture, explains that, from now on, every plot of land should be about "and" rather than just "or." He goes on to talk geranium and pineapple, sugar and coffee, orange and tangerine, presenting agriculture as a vast mosaic of vegetables, spices, and fruit that they must all create together.

Henceforth, it will be do or die. Polyculture, or pack up and go. Additional crops, or the stern of a three-master sailing straight back to Lorient.

"Here is the pod of vanilla that will change your destiny and that of the island of Bourbon! We have vanilla creepers and flowers, but ever since the plant arrived here, it has given us no fruit. Who, out of all of you, will find that fruit? Who will volunteer to plant vanilla? Who wants to be rich and famous in this land of paupers?" asks Cuvillier.

"Two hectares of land and a cutting to every man who doesn't say no," he declares.

Ferréol, with a four-year-old Edmond in his arms, listens attentively. Without a second's hesitation, he, botanist, horticulturalist, naturalist, green-foliage obsessive and self-proclaimed orchid specialist, lifts up his head, raises a finger, then his whole hand, jumps up and down, buzzing with questions. He hasn't yet found the orchid of his dreams, maybe he'll find something just as good, if not better: the rarest fruit!

"Planting's fine, but how? Over how many years? Where are they, these hectares?"

He's barely had time to ask his first question, hand still aloft, before he discovers Edmond's little hand gripping a cutting attached to a stake stuck in a hat filled with soil. And that's how, in Ferréol's garden at Bellevue, in Sainte-Suzanne, one of the rare vanilla plants in the history of Bourbon is replanted. According to his friend, Mézières Lepervanche, vanilla was only grown in the gardens of a few amateurs at that time.

This story of vanilla, from the Aztec forests to the neighborhood of Bellevue, via Gibraltar and the Andalusian plains, has been listened to, religiously, by an open-mouthed Edmond since he was four years, seven months, and several cyclones old. Every evening, Edmond requests the same tale of the familiar odyssey, which fills out over time; each evening, he draws a map in his head for the wayfaring orchid, from Veracruz to La Guyane to Versailles, and even to the lazaret at the Ravine-à-Jacques. Ferréol then launches into a monologue, sprinkled with myths and flights of fancy, about an extraordinary plant with twenty-meter-long stems, thick leaves, and pale blooms that survive but a day. But this story takes a new turn when the eight-year-old Edmond learns that vanilla had borne fruit in Belgium, the previous year, thanks to Charles Morren. This year, it's a French botanist, Joseph Neuman, who has succeeded in pollinating vanilla. In both cases, the maneuver is so complex, so obscure, that the initiators themselves struggle to reproduce it; it doesn't catch on, seldom be repeated. But for Edmond, who stares wide-eyed, just a single fact matters: vanilla can bear fruit outside of Mexico! It's within the realm of the possible, not just the world of dreams! And that's how he becomes obsessed with vanilla, addicted to an orphan creeper that crossed half the globe between four small panels of wood. Edmond loves the story of this orchid so much, he wants to be the one to unlock the plant's secret. Like those little girls who, after listening to too many tales of prince charming, dream only of a princess's tiara, but end up, at best, as servants in the kitchens of a palace. Ferréol, who now speaks a lot but no longer listens, is unaware of the storm brewing in the head of his little Creole Linnaeus, of his own personal quest for the rarest fruit. Or rather, he brushes away like flies, with the back of his hand, Edmond's impudent desires, the gall of his youth, that singular temerity that makes him talk in his sleep, dangle from branches, and jump off the roof if no one's watching over him.

10
THE VANILLA FLOWERS
Bellevue, 1837-1840

Sometimes making the sound of a hen, sometimes that of a mouse rummaging in a pile of dry leaves, he goads the vanilla flowers, his hands covered in pollen.

For four years now, Ferréol has owned a vanilla plant. For four years now, Edmond has regularly observed, by day, this ornamental plant whose story he's told at night. When he's in the cane fields, with this bunch of living skeletons that make up his family—men with bruised skin holding a machete or a pitchfork, solemn and silent women, old at barely thirty-five—he tells them all about vanilla, Charles Morren's discovery, the life of wild orchids. They are all amazed—some would say annoyed—at the chattiness of this child who's so similar yet so different from them, and perky as a parrot.

Where does he get this youthfulness, this unfamiliar freshness from? Did his mother have it? Much as they, too, try to reassemble the scattered jigsaw pieces of their memory, they can no long remember his parents.

On washing Sundays, beside the river Sainte-Suzanne, Edmond bores Isidore stiff with his tedious, never-ending story of vanilla and its latest Belgian, and then French, development. If Charles Morren is right, vanilla flowers are the most ephemeral flowers that Edmond, Ferréol, and even Isidore know of. Ephemeral because they wilt at the close of just a single day. At least three months of patience before a vanilla plant produces its first flowers. Three-and-a-half months, from September to December, during which the vanilla plant flowers. A lifespan of just one day for each bloom, so barely twelve hours in which to pollinate it. And even then, if it's very warm, the flower closes and dies before the end of the afternoon. At least six weeks of waiting, if the pollination is successful, for the pod of vanilla to reach its maximum size. Nine more months for it to be ripe and ready to be picked. In total, almost a year between pollination and the harvesting of the ripe fruit. Isidore reckons that, in terms of troublesome plants, Edmond would struggle to find worse. Edmond replies that, when it comes to rare fruit, he'd struggle to find better. Bright-eyed, curious, smart as an octopus and very focused, Edmond doesn't agree with that killjoy Isidore. He's used to the worst, he was born with it. His existence was turned upside down in one minute and forty-six seconds. So twelve hours to make a mark on the history of Bourbon, it's almost too long. He wagers that between him and that fob watch Ferréol wears—a gift from the late Angélique at a time when she didn't totally loathe him—it is he who'll win this race before the twilight of his life.

Edmond is nine and a few months when, for the first time, he watches Ferréol attempting to pollinate what, until then, had just been an ornamental plant that flowered for three months of the year at the edge of his orchid nursery.

It's decided, Ferréol will proceed just the way he does with pumpkins. He handles some of the delicate flowers with relish, even talks to them a little. Patience, dexterity. Supple and gentle hand movements. That's all he ever talks about. Beside him, Edmond, solemn and meticulous as an alchemist, holds a bodkin or a diaper pin.

Sometimes making the sound of a hen, sometimes that of a mouse rummaging in a pile of dry leaves, Ferréol goads the vanilla flowers; he turns over the leaves, unties the tangled stalks, folds them back, starts again. He keeps trying to pollinate the flowers until nightfall, fast, faster, before they die, so that in a year's time, the fruit can be picked. He returns, with Edmond, the following day at dawn.

"Hand me the clip, Edmond. I can feel it, this time it's going to work."

"*V'là, lé là, ti père.*"—Here it is, Daddy.

The day after, Ferréol is more pumped up with optimism than the day before. Leaning forward, Edmond gets his annual lesson in plant anatomy from his *ti père* over a trembling liana. Ferréol indicates what he thinks is a pistil and, looking authoritative, repeats to Edmond for the eight-hundredth time that it's on this ovary that grains of pollen from the stamen must be placed. He takes the one, brings over the other, is sure of nothing, doubts everything, suddenly battling with imaginary bees. Tomorrow we'll get there!

The day after that, Edmond is so bored he hunts for snails, then teases the sensitive ones, while Ferréol turns the vanilla flowers in all directions.

During the three months of flowering, with Edmond watching, Ferréol fingers, coaxes, trisects, so that towards December, the first fruit will appear.

From the murky depths where his happiness languishes, Ferréol thinks he can smell the sweet aroma of vanilla, allows it to reach his nostrils, his eyelids, and finally his slowed-down heart, which returns to beating like a drum. He can't be sure of it, but it does seem that he's happy.

On January 1, 1839, Edmond wakes up as usual at six, takes Ferréol his coffee, and gets ready to go and inspect the vanilla nursery with him. If the Belgian botanist Charles Morren was right, the first vanilla pods should already be waiting impatiently. Instead of the usual red dirt track that snakes its way to the vanilla plant, he feels as if he's walking on a path strewn with clover. Ferréol skips along, rubbing his hands, eyes sparkling, belief in his heart. As soon as he arrives, he's disillusioned, like the day when, on her deathbed, Angélique told him that she'd never wanted to marry him because . . . This admission in an unfinished sentence had punched a hole in him wide as a crater, making him lose his voice and sleep. After that, he'd never wanted to marry again, hear the breathing of a woman in his bed again, see a dress lying on a chair again. He'd gone back to collecting orchids.

All the same, Ferréol stands before the vanilla creeper and confines himself to groaning. Between the clear blue sky and the dew-drenched earth, nothing. Not a single fruit. It was all too good to be true. He returns to the house and discovers, in his newspaper, that that habitual offender Dumas is bringing out an *opéra comique*. It won't be on in Bourbon any time soon. Ferréol folds up the paper, throws it onto the table, and goes back to bed to forget everything. He sleeps without snoring, arm resting on belly, head buried in pillow. A week later, still nothing. Not a single pod. Ferréol reddens, surrounded by the stakes. All the flowers have gone, along with his illusions.

The weeks, months, years go by. Ferréol comes and goes on his plots of land, plants some Mysore trumpet vines, some bois de gaulette, some tiger lilies, and, from time to time, inspects his vanilla nursery. He knows only too well that, at every flowering, this vanilla is the only one of his orchids to put him into a dreadful state. It persists in not producing any fruit. And it's already December 1840! He can't believe it. How time flies! To think that he's owned his vanilla plant since 1833. Since that's how it is, it can just stay right there, with its accursed flowers that serve no purpose.

"A vulgar ornamental plant, nothing more!" he laments, slamming the *baro* of his nursery.

Each year, Edmond scratches his head, too; all that remains is the great void of chance, and its mechanism has jammed. There's an element of this vanilla business that escapes him. One evening, he thinks hard about it. This waiting can't go on any longer. If the vanilla flower can't produce fruit on its own, without a helping hand, I, Edmond, will happily lend it both of my hands.

11
FRUITLESS ATTEMPTS
1841, *annus horribilis*

Still nothing.

1841. Edmond is twelve, with maybe a touch of acne. On Elvire's veranda, where Ferréol and his old friend Eugène Volcy-Focard are starting their game of Boston, Edmond hears them talk of the innovations, of the surge of changes progressively sweeping away the bygones of his childhood. First, in Sainte-Suzanne, everyone's talking about the building of a lighthouse, twenty meters tall and with seventy steps, costing ten thousand francs. Then, in the rest of the island of Bourbon, the Governor has officially decreed that the Blacks, who usually come and go naked as worms from the waist up, can no longer circulate without being fittingly clad, the men in shirt and trousers, the women in a dress, or blouse and petticoat. For shoes, they'll make do, as usual, with the soles of their feet. And finally, apparently a visitor, a lad of twenty, but not any lad, Baudelaire himself, has settled—for around forty days—in Salazie, where Ferréol owns land. It's so rare, a foreigner in this Cirque, that all the landowners and stewards, including Ferréol's at Terre-Plate, are talking about it and spreading tittle-tattle. The writer Eugène Crépet quotes the poet Théodore de Banville, who, having gotten wind of this news, would hastily recounted it in his *Souvenirs*. Baudelaire, then "lodging with a family to whom his parents had sent him, had soon found the banality of his hosts boring, and had gone off to live alone on a mountain, with a very young, tall girl of color who spoke no French, and would cook him strangely spiced stews in a large cauldron of polished copper, around which naked little piccaninnies would dance."[10]

Maybe the young Baudelaire reignites Ferréol's old literary dream. Whatever the reason, it's that year that Ferréol begins to compile a dictionary of the fruit trees of Bourbon, in which he writes a detailed description of all the species he has encountered. Three hundred species of flower recorded, as many trees, eighty-seven footnotes, an endeavor so notable that it will give him every right to establish the Botanical Society of Bourbon, his new great secret dream, and maybe to give his name to an endemic species of tree fern, his third secret dream.

Edmond, who isn't the right color to have vocations or read poems, merely reflects that it's been ages since he last set foot in the vanilla nursery, where flowering has begun. A few days later, armed with his cane-cutting machete and a satchel full of biscuits and some dried meat taken from the storeroom, he rolls up his trousers and the sleeves of his jacket, and heads off to Ferréol's vanilla plants. He crosses a track lined with Peruvian pepper trees, their pink peppercorns hanging in bunches above his head, greets a row of slaves he hasn't seen for some time, and reaches the plot, when he lets out a cry of astonishment. In front of him, there's a thick tangle of creepers that are climbing the length of the fences, stretching from mango tree to mango tree, winding around the bushes like an orgy of grass snakes, and blocking the track that leads to the fields of guava trees. Above all, there are several flowers—light yellow, pale yellow, delicate green, soft green, chayote green—adorning every creeper. Edmond hunts for pods like a vagabond for treasure; he finds not a single one.

---

[10] *Charles Baudelaire—Étude biographique*, by Eugène Crépet, revised and updated by Jacques Crépet, followed by *Baudelairiana d'Asselineau*, Paris, Librairie Léon Vanier, 1906.

He heads back to the house, again passing the row of slaves, who gently mock him; he promises them that tomorrow, yes, tomorrow, he'll perform miracles in that vanilla nursery, when he hasn't the first reason to say that. The wind shakes the treetops, the first rain of the season begins to fall. Plop, plop. Edmond walks in the mud, makes his way through the maze of puddles. Tomorrow, yes, tomorrow, he'll accomplish a feat just as showy as that planned lighthouse. What a witless thing to say! He admits it himself. But this desire remains lodged in his head like a nail. If he doesn't manage to do it, or if Ferréol stops him, he'll crush all the flowers, a whole vanilla plant, in anger!

From the following Monday, Edmond comes and goes in the morning breezes, the first warmth after winter, the afternoon downpours. In the fields, from where they observe Edmond's daily toing and froing, the slaves, their curiosity piqued, start betting, to win a bigger bit of bread: will find it, won't find it? Edmond has studied enough flowers, pollinated enough pumpkins all his short life, to distinguish, eyes closed, the male organ, the stamen, from the female organ, the pistil, and put the two together. From first light every morning, while Ferréol dreams he's a great *Encyclopédiste*, Edmond goes off to fiddle with the vanilla flowers before they die in the late afternoon.

Week one. The vanilla is in flower, and Edmond in a trance. From six in the morning, he fiddles with, coaxes, fingers the petals, then waits, turns pale, chats with Isidore, until the shedding of the final vanilla flower at dusk signals the end of that round.

Week Two. Other vanilla-plant stems are in flower, and Edmond's in a frenzy. Until one o'clock, he's still on the job, fondling, manipulating, maneuvering, conniving, pimping a plant coitus between stamen and pistil, before the eyes of a few ladybugs and before Grand-Marron, who prefers to turn his eyes away.

Week three. Here we go again. Some creepers are in flower, Edmond's in ecstasy. Once more, all day long, he feels, gropes, teases, taps, while nearby, Colombine is seriously wondering about his mental health.

Day twenty-three. The vanilla is in flower, Edmond in a rage. It's already today! He can't believe it. God, how time races by, like a hare!

He's on water duty, must tidy the kitchen garden, feed the hens. He won't be able to finger any vanilla flowers today.

Day twenty-seven. The vanilla is in flower, Edmond in a panic. He keeps making clumsy slips, crushes dozens of petals, feels disheartened, loses his temper with himself, finally gives up.

Day twenty-nine. The vanilla is in flower, Edmond on alert. The end of the season is approaching. It's raining cats and dogs. The soil is now an impossible sludge in which he flounders, slips, almost sprains his ankle. From her veranda, Elvire urges him to stop playing at frogs and come home right now. There's some tart left over from breakfast. The vanilla can wait until tomorrow. As for fruit, there's still none.

We don't know what Ferréol is doing all this time. We don't know whether he's still writing his encyclopedia. We just know that he isn't there. Considering the previous attempts, Edmond thinks that, anyhow, it's better that way.

12
Vanilla Planifolia
1841, a lucky year

*With his nose covered in pollen,
he cried out with joy: I've got it!*

Summer 1841. Between the Marine neighborhood of Sainte-Suzanne and the Quartier-Français, something's not right. In the field belonging to Charles Gélase, doctor and botanist, the cattle are waiting for their bales of straw beside empty carts, the dry washing is still hanging on the line. In the distance, the smoke from the Bois-Rouge sugar factory is but a barely visible wisp. On the banks of the Grande Rivière Saint-Jean, a heap of undershirts, crinoline petticoats, and corsets is gradually diminishing as garments slide off the rocks, taking on the breadth of the ravine as they head for the sea. The riverbanks are missing the usual singing of the washerwomen. Monsieur Gélase is perplexed; two slices of bread smeared with jam and a jug of water sit on his breakfast table, but no coffee or tea. Not a single slave, or the least maidservant now, anywhere to be seen.

Only that fellow called Serpent, a slave freed last year for revealing a conspiracy, informs him that they're all at the Hauts de Bellevue, where Ferréol has his vanilla nursery. Even the old diviner, the *devinèr,* has hastened there, the one known as "the man of the night." Outside, some landowners are deliberating. There's Urbain Léon, once a lieutenant commander on a corvette, who came via Madagascar, Cayenne and Dakar. There's the engineer Stanislas Pierre Séverat, inventor of a procedure to facilitate sugar production. And there's Antoine Grégoire, who's said to have fainted after saying "yes" at his wedding. Through their telescope, the masters observe a small gathering up there, in Bellevue; Ferréol, meanwhile, is just preparing his quill pen and inkpot.

Several slaves from Sainte-Suzanne stand in a ring, looking out for Edmond, that little companion who always helps them finish a chore. When you're threatened with the whip if the corn isn't harvested in time, you call Edmond, he pitches in to get it done. When you're dying of thirst, Edmond brings a mug of water under the steward's very nose. When you miss a day's work, Edmond finds any pretext so the culprit avoids a whipping with the *chabouk*. They know that Edmond has been searching for weeks, months, a few years, for the secret of some orchid; they've decided to come and support him, once and for all.

At around six on the first day of October, Edmond arrives, once again, at the vanilla nursery. For a few years now, it has been a rectangular plot under glass, with eight paths and seven rows of stakes, a huge refectory serving fleshy leaves that the snails relish, and with ants dashing around everywhere. To his great surprise, a dozen or so slaves are there, waiting for him, sitting against the stakes or, a bit further along, under the Indian laurels, or leaning on the Song of India trees. They're sure he's going to find what he's looking for, even if they don't really know what it is. Edmond, at first timid, disconcerted, then, finally, excited, approaches a vanilla flower. He tries, turns, repeats ten, twenty, thirty times. Around him, all the slaves watch. Edmond moves on to another flower, seeks and lifts, separates, then brings together. On his fingers, pollen; in his hands, petals. The slaves at the back, too far to see a thing, make do with what details the front-row spectators relay to them. Those in front watch him, puzzled, wondering when he'll finish this strange rigmarole. A bored child yawns, his mother instantly shakes him; two day-laborers comment on the slanting rain, which they all find really beautiful. The wait seems endless to them.

Suddenly, Edmond straightens up and smiles. The slaves immediately hold their breath. False alert!

Edmond tries, and tries, and tries again without getting anywhere.

In front of him, behind, all around, the slaves resume their muttering. A bit of support, dammit! Suddenly, all you can hear is one loud voice, formed of twelve separate voices out of twelve different mouths chanting the same name in the Bellevue vanilla nursery: Edmond! Edmond! Edmond!

Surprised by this enthusiastic crowd, Edmond gets back to it, like he did yesterday, two weeks ago, a month ago. Both the same way and differently. In front of all these smiling souls, their feet pressed to the ground, bodies still, eyes shining, these folks waiting, mouths agape, Edmond can feel himself growing wings of Icarus that will enable him to touch the sun. Yet another myth, this time Greek, that Ferréol told him! He tries some more. For his mother who is watching. For his father who, wherever he is, is hoping. For his brothers here who are waiting. He feels the anxiety of the pupil three seconds before exam results are announced, the hope of the priest who knocks on Heaven's door not knowing whether God will open it. Edmond and forty others hope, but don't know.

Suddenly, he's thinking. Suddenly, he loses heart. Suddenly, he crumples.

He's Black, and he's poor, and he's an orphan, and . . . And what the hell!

Considering that, in three months and twelve years, he's seen it all—that the dung enriches the soil, that it's a potent organic stimulant, that thanks to it, the banana tree, breadfruit tree, geranium, *Brunfelsia*, and periwinkle all flourish—he thinks maybe it's not so bad that he's up to his neck in shit. Edmond feels the breeze on his cheeks, a light sea breeze. Gradually, it turns into a wind of anger, of revenge, of revolt. A voice somewhere, maybe inside him, tells him: Edmond, don't give up. Another voice, from the back of the vanilla nursery, cries out:

Edmond, enter here! Take what is not yours!

The mutterings say it's the old healer, who usually thinks he's God, who spoke. Maybe it's the other way round. At that moment, a little black-and-white beetle, a *bébête l'argent*—money bug—a symbol of success, of fortune around these parts, flies above Edmond's head, suddenly drops, as if in an air pocket, tips to the right, then to the left, and finally settles on his shoulder, as oohs and aahs of wonderment rise up.

"It's a sign!" they shout.

At twelve years old and no specific time, Edmond's heart starts beating again. Twelve years and a bodkin, he reopens his eyes, looks closely, feels remarkably dim not to have understood a thing. Twelve years and two needles, in the searing heat, Edmond gesticulates when the others pray, cries out when they go quiet, freezes as soon as they grow impatient. From this febrile tropical discord, the familiar words Ferréol taught him break through. Flower. Pollen sac. Pistil, female organ. Stamen, male organ. Make pistil and stamen touch each other.

"Is it coming?"

"No, it isn't coming."

Time goes by and anxiety grips the slaves. They huddle together like chicks in straw. They form a chain of unity, joined by a few butterflies, two or three ladybugs, a good deal of hope.

In the middle of this living circle, Edmond, clad in a beige linen smock, feels a renewed optimism.

"And now, is it coming?"

"No, still not. Still not since 1519. Still not since 1833."

Edmond moves his eyes closer, even closer, to a flower. He

begins to understand. In the vanilla flower, there's a natural obstacle, like a little door, the rostellum, separating the male organ from the female organ. This fine membrane, this delicate protective hymen, prevents any pollination. With the help of a splinter of bamboo, Edmond lifts this operculum, opens the little door. With this thin covering moved aside, he puts the stamen, the male organ full of pollen, into contact with the female organ. The vanilla flower is pollinated.

This time it is going to work, he knows it. He touches and moves aside, lifts and deposits. And, with his nose covered in pollen, Edmond lets out the cry of a scientist:

I've got it!

A tremendous discovery in eight minutes, twelve years—four thousand three hundred and eighty days—and three centuries, there in Bellevue, that's to say, nowhere. And yet no one sees the miracle. The slaves around Edmond haven't really understood any of it. Before the flabbergasted crowd, it's the same Edmond, the same silent orchid plant, the same flower. Maybe a tiny trace of something resembling pollen on a minuscule thingamajig a bit like a thorn. The slaves closest by saw him uncovering a something-or-other to deposit some didn't-really-see-what there. Like for the pumpkins.

But Edmond is so sure of himself that they believe him. Like for the pumpkins. Eugène Volcy-Focard confirmed it later on when he wrote that Edmond's constant observing of pumpkins had led him to attempt the same procedure on vanilla.

In the vanilla nursery, everyone can breathe again. They are all talking loudly and saying that Ferréol is right: vanilla is just a pumpkin like any other. Having established this, they each return to their fields, where the stewards of the likes of Grégoire, Séverat, and Gélase await them, *chabouk* in hand, stamping their feet. But it's no good. When they see them returning in such large numbers, they fear mutiny, lower their horsewhips and leave them be, for that day. The riding-crop gymnastics can wait until tomorrow.

Edmond returns to Ferréol's house, smiling. Like with pumpkins, he'll have to wait until the first fruit appears.

Waiting, that's all he's done all his life, he's used to it.

Five weeks later, Edmond is walking through Ferréol's vanilla nursery when he discovers a firm pod, apple-green in color, two-fingers long. It looks like a runner bean, or his third finger. Edmond knows it, this is the very first vanilla pod of the island of Bourbon. Of the Indian Ocean. Born of a flower he pollinated. Poised to shake up Bourbon's agricultural economy. So this is the rarest fruit in the world! So this is what a tornado looks like? A rigid caterpillar!

Malicious gossips claim that, in vengeful anger against Ferréol, Edmond had crushed the flowers. Others say he discovered how to do it unintentionally; when climbing a tree he wanted to sleep in all day, his feet—not even his hands—supposedly crushed the vanilla flowers, thus pollinating a few among them. In short, he didn't try at all, and has barely any merit. That's the malicious gossips, and there are plenty of those around him.

Maybe he was alone, totally alone, facing his destiny in the vanilla nursery. Maybe that story about slaves coming to encourage him is but the inspired fantasy of a suddenly lonely apprentice botanist. What do the maybes and the gossips matter? What's most important, anyway, lies elsewhere.

His name is Edmond. He's twelve years old. In a 19th century dull as dishwater, in which people eat what's practical, far from concerned about the taste, presentation, or flavor of food, Edmond has just produced a new spice. In a century, then, in which folks are only used to two tastes, the bitterness of margoses and the sharpness of key limes; in which cane sugar is rare; a century, as we were saying, in which sweet potato, bread, and heartburn triumph, he, Edmund, twelve years old, brings to the western world a new taste, a flavor forgotten since the 16th century. The flavor of vanilla.

13
Edmond Tells Ferréol
the Incredible News
The vanilla nursery, late 1841

"I no longer recalled this teaching when, that same year at the latest, walking with my faithful companion, I spotted, on the only vanilla plant I owned at the time, a fully developed pod. I was amazed and pointed it out to him. He told me that it was he who had pollinated the flower. I refused to believe it." —
Letter from Ferréol Bellier-Beaumont to the magistrate of Sainte-Suzanne, February 17, 1861[11]

On the third Sunday of October, 1841, Ferréol is strolling through his Bellevue orchards with Edmond when he witnesses a miracle. Before his eyes, the impossible becomes reality; he shakes his head, rubs his eyes; nothing changes. He sees a pod that's green as a bean, with a thick skin, not a bit fragile. Feverish as a pirate unearthing treasure, he takes in the smallest details. He wonders out loud how such a thing could have happened like this, after eight years of nothing. Edmond says it was he who pollinated the flower, as if it was, indeed, nothing. He explains and describes, while fluttering his fingers. Ferréol puts on his most serious expression, then bursts out laughing, for the third time in forty-nine years. This joke from that rascal Edmond, a born joker, comes at just the right time, relaxing him.

But joking aside, how on earth can such a wonder have come about? And Edmond repeats: "It was me, *ti père!*" Ferréol's laughter has already given way to slight impatience. The shortest jokes are the funniest. He resumes his serious and sullen look, the one he has on his great thinking days. These last few months, he has noticed a great many bees, beetles, and the native stonechats, *tec-tecs,* in his fields. It must be that. Edmond listens to him, shaking his

---

[11] *Archives de Bourbon no. 10.*

head. He's very proud of his *ti père*, but, may God forgive him, he does sometimes find him a bit of a goose. It's not his fault, it's that of this lousy world that deals the wrong cards, making some kings and queens full of confidence, others mere jacks armed with pick-axes in cane fields. At this, Edmond sighs; he understands Ferréol. His inability to doubt himself, his ability to doubt everyone else, his fear of losing status, of mutinies, of all the traps he's laid himself, which, gradually, are closing up on him.

Edmond keeps his patience as tightly tied as the bundle of straw he's carrying.

"*C'est moin missié, mi jure.*"—It was me, *monsieur*, I swear.

He only says "*monsieur*" at the most serious moments, when Ferréol is scolding him, and other slaves running away, as if such sudden deference would diffuse Ferréol's anger and wrap things up.

Ferréol isn't listening to anything. Cardinal birds, with their scarlet heads, red plumage, round bellies, coal-black eyes, perch on top of the stakes and watch with curiosity. They love a good scrap and are enjoying every minute.

"The secret of this orchid, which neither local botanists, nor those at the natural history museum in Paris, have managed to unlock, has been unlocked by a little Black boy? Really? The feat a Belgian once achieved, without even managing to repeat it, without anyone even managing to imitate him, with one chance in a hundred of working, a child has solved the mystery? Really?! A slave of twelve! Really?!"

And Ferréol gets annoyed at Edmond's insistence, even though it's from his *ti père* that Edmond gets this trait. He resumes his walk and describes what ensued in a letter: "Two or three days later, I see a second pod beside the first one. And he just repeats his claim to me."[12]

---

[12] *Archives de Bourbon no. 10*, letter from Ferréol Bellier-Beaumont to the magistrate of Sainte-Suzanne, February 17, 1861.

"If you did it, do it again in front of me."

Edmond puts down his bundle, cursing inside, and goes ahead.

"Is that it? Just that? And now go fetch me more bundles of straw."

Ferréol tells him to meet him there, same time, same flower, ten days later, and promises him the thrashing of the century. But right now, he feels like neither staying put, nor going home. He tarries in the fields, from which he hears the bell ringing for recess at the tiny school Elvire has run for a few weeks now, for the little girls of the neighborhood. Ferréol wanders on, paying no attention to Rose and Lilas, who are shrieking as they escape from their wooden bench. Level with his waist, Hévéa is smuggling in gingerbread and bobbins of wool from a young mulatto; Beaumont doesn't see her. Any more than he sees the clog-throwing contest, which very nearly shatters his skull. He's cogitating, hesitating, scratching the nape of his neck, muttering to himself, surrounded by three little girls waddling around like geese.

For nine nights, Ferréol can't sleep, overwhelmed at the thought of what has happened, excited at the thought of what might happen. He talks to Elvire, who doesn't understand a word, busy as she is cosseting three girls whose parents don't want them.

On the morning of the tenth day, Edmond is nowhere to be found. Ferréol goes off to the orchard on his own. Near his only vanilla plant, Edmond is waiting and smiling. Where nine days ago there was a flower, there's now a new, fully developed pod. Quite small, certainly. But well and truly there. Who? How? And Edmond says again: *C'est moin, ti père. Depuis tout le temps que mi dit a ou sa*!—It was me, *ti père*. As I've long been telling you! Well, do it again! Edmond goes ahead. A meeting is fixed for ten days' time. Ferréol returns, sees. He doubts. Do it again! As the days go by, new pods appear once Edmond has hand-pollinated the flowers. Again!

The refrain continues until there's not a single flower left to pollinate, until there's only fruit to be seen. Now, Ferréol is convinced. One morning, in front of all these creepers from which pods long as green beans hang, he hugs Edmond, kisses him, does an excited little jig, as if at carnival, and keeps saying alleluia, so relieved and euphoric is he.

"The rarest fruit," he repeats to Edmond. "The rarest!"

He rewards Edmond with a slap on the back so vigorous, so enthusiastic, he almost dislocates the boy's shoulder. Ferréol forgets everything—the smell of bean stew wafting over from the house, Grand-Marron spying on him, the thousand concerns of a colonist's life, maintaining rank when faced with questioning slaves. He's swept up by a wave of unknown emotions. And this excess of heartbeats, shouting, shock turns into a tremor across his eyelashes, cheeks, moustache, mouth. His whole face contorts, shrinks, lengthens, until flooded with the tears of an excited young man, bawling and bawling with resounding joy. As for Edmond, he tries to console Ferréol by holding his great hairy paws in his own small ebony hands. *Ah ben, ti père, plèr pa comme sa*—Hey, *ti père*, don't cry like that. But suddenly, he, too, can feel two trickles of something falling from his eyes. With neither now being able to reason with the other, they hold each other by the shoulders and cry so hard that, at their feet, a little pool of tears forms, which some toads already have their eyes on.

For the first time in his life, Ferréol returns home really happy, so proud that such an important discovery has been made on his estate. As the days go by, it seems normal to him that the method for hand-pollinating vanilla should have been discovered thanks to him.

He remembers all that he patiently taught Edmond. He recalls the botanical expeditions he'd return from empty-handed, with three miserable guava leaves in the *bertelle* [13] that serves

---

[13] Knapsack made of vacoa fiber.

him as a sample bag. He sees again the cyclones that destroyed his crops and nursery, the incendiary accusations of Angélique, who swore he'd never make anything of his life and would end up a potato-picker or refinery janitor.

This rare fruit of an orchid that's equally rare is simply fair compensation for his past efforts.

One starless night, before retiring to bed, he suddenly sits up and thinks. He must add an entry for "vanilla" to his encyclopedia, adjoining Edmond's name to it, a slave of barely twelve, a Cafre, an all-in-one—gardener-bee-botanist-orphan-illiterate— who discovered almost single-handedly how to hand-pollinate vanilla. He'd have to inform the newspapers, explain in their columns how one creates this fruit that's so rare, and admit— dammit, he'd not thought of that at all—that he, Ferréol, wasn't present on that particular day. The journalists would surely want to question Edmond, get a watercolor portrait done of him. He must get his hair cut, his toenails, too. All the vanilla growers will certainly ask to meet him. He must be thanked.

The following day, reluctantly, barely moving his lips, he says: "Not bad, Edmond. Have the day off!" He thinks: Lord, why him?

14
FERRÉOL AS PATIENT
The sickbed, 1842

Ferréol is dying of some unknown disease contracted in his orchard where dozens of green pods are hanging.

At the start of the year 1842, the second act begins of the tragicomedy that Edmond's life becomes. In addition to the trade winds, a fresh wind of modernity still blows on the island: in Sainte-Rose, a new suspension bridge is planned to span the river in the east of the island, and a bridle path is now open between Saint-Louis and the Cilaos Cirque. Everywhere there are new sugar refineries, roads, bridges. Only the bascule bridge that would connect owners and slaves remains permanently raised: the Colonial Council refuses point-blank all proposals for the abolition of slavery. Busy with his usual gardening work after the vanilla season, Edmond feels a twinge of sorrow when he learns that emancipation isn't happening anytime soon. It's not for himself that he worries, he has nothing to complain about. It's for Isidore and all the others whose lives, from the baptistry to the grave, consist merely of zigzagging between coffee trees and cocoa trees, clove trees and cornfields, cassava and potatoes, tubers like the white-fleshed *songes* and the mauve *cambarres*, beans and sugarcane. And all that without even eating their fill.

Edmond is concerned about the others without noticing that his own world is starting to crumble like a *pâté créole*—that lard-and-saffron pie, dense and dry as a brick, a real granny-choker he usually tucks into at the start of the year with a tot of rum.

February 1842. A great commotion is shaking the upper floor of the house at Belleville. Ferréol's neighbors are gathered around his four-poster bed, while his brothers and sisters are dabbing their eyes with monogrammed handkerchiefs. In the sky, the clouds are gathering. Everywhere, the same scenario: an atmosphere heavy as a barricade. Edmond hears the rumor without being able to confirm it: Ferréol is dying of some unknown disease contracted in his orchard where dozens of green pods are hanging that no one has ever seen before. Outside, the pods are thriving; in his bed, Ferréol is dying.

The slaves hear the yelps of a sick animal, imagine that their master is going to die, and laugh with delight. Because that's the way of the world. Because a half-full bowl and a longer chain don't equal freedom.

All the doctors on the island are consulted. In vain. Now, from every boat that berths at Bourbon, some medic alights and is ushered by porters straight to the Beaumonts' place. On the dew-darkened paving stones, Edmond now hears only the hooves of horses, the wheels of carioles passing the kitchens, the hurried steps of friends quietly asking Elvire the way to the patient's room. In the corridors, a bunch of priests, sorcerers, quacks, and doctors eye each other scornfully as they come and go. Under woolen covers, Ferréol curls up like a snake biting its own tail, with four leeches in the hollow of his stomach, a poultice on his forehead. He complains of an unspeakable pain, implores God to come by again. At the four corners of his bed, a small crucifix, some goat hairs, volcanic salt, and verbena. An impressive medley of charms, their smell fouling up the air.

Between his sheets, Ferréol now veers from fits of laughter, to tears, to nerves. In his nightmares, he speaks of an Edmond whose discovery is an obstacle to his own honor. His father was an officer of the Volontaires de Bourbon, an equerry, whereas he, Ferréol, has done nothing. A Black, his own pupil, discovering vanilla! What a triumph for Edmond!

Under that roof, the rivalry between the two of them begins, the ambiguity of the father-son relationship. In the garden, Edmond now looks after the orchids on his own.

In the rattan-furnished sitting room, where the region's biggest landowners are seated, shoes tap on the black-and-white checkered floor. Tongues loosen.

"They say it's that brat over there who put Ferréol into this state."

"Apparently, he's just discovered the secret of vanilla."

"Who has? That stripling reading in front of the tree nursery?"

"No, come now! That's my son, Henri-Baptiste!"

"Which one then?"

"The mulatto in the jacket, just behind the nursery, near the mill and those poinsettias?"

"No way. He's called Isidore."

"Enough now, which one?"

"That other one, the last one. The Black slave watering the orchids and maidenhair ferns."

"Good grief! That ugly creature can't possibly have pollinated vanilla!"

And the father of Henri-Baptiste almost chokes over his cup of tea.

A wealthy colonist speaks of the breach into which all slaves are now going to step because of this Edmond. It threatens their very traditions, the monopoly of power so hard-won with crowbars in the 17th century. Another landowner blanches with shame, speaks of insult and humiliation. Upstairs, Ferréol falls out of bed and his fragile pride goes with him; he recovers from the first, gives up on the second. Outdoors, Isidore has stopped saying that Edmond is white. Ferréol finds himself alone, frothing at the mouth, a glint in his eye. Today, let them speak to him about anyone, all humanity, except Edmond!

Soon, the rumor spreads across the island and in the local

press. Monsieur Beaumont's suffering is so great, he will hand over two thousand francs to any man who brings him an effective remedy. Edmond knocks timidly on his door. He's missing his *ti père* and is worried about his health. He's bringing him a decoction of ayapana and chamomile flowers, picked fresh in his kitchen garden.

"Not him!" is heard, shouted from between the pillows.

Colombine chases Edmond away vigorously with her broom and lowers the wooden bar across the sturdy front door.

How come, not him? Edmond doesn't understand. Him, the little Black boy who made the ingenious discovery—Ferréol's description—is suddenly *persona non grata*. Him, the *ti gâté pourri*? It can only be a misunderstanding, which, thanks to his nearly thirteen years of optimism, dexterity, and diplomacy, he'll soon sort out. In the meantime, Grand-Marron indicates to him the stone *calbanon* in which, for the first time tonight, he will sleep with the other slaves.

Outside, a small group of Blacks who've never liked him are gloating. The rumor's picked up speed. Your master's really mad at you. So you wanted to have everything all at once, you greedy pig, you filthy *goulapia*?[14] To be a slave *and* the son of a White man? They say *missié* Ferréol's going to send you away like a bale of rice, to his place at Terre-Plate. Richard's stewards make fun of Edmond, that future exile for good behavior. They can already picture him on that *îlet*, that remote plateau with cats everywhere, aphids, rats, nettles that sting and scratch. They turn it into a story, telling it to the other slaves, while they strip the dry leaves from the cane, as a warning. It consoles them for their extreme misery that Edmond should suffer a little. That's what happens to those who aren't satisfied with their lot! They end up thinner, arms peeling, digging stony ground all on their own.

[14] A gourmand.

Crime or no crime, he's guilty!

Edmond, who never knew people could smile so much at him while hating him behind his back, feels it like a sledge-hammer blow to the head, a dagger in his back planted by Isidore when he tells him he's sold his soul to the Whites. But he doesn't cry. As soon as he's back on his feet, Ferréol will sort out this misunderstanding himself. Edmond also knows what his parents think of all this. He looks up at the stars and can make out their smiles and blessings from a paradise planted with green orchids.

In the distance, above the sea, the clouds are gathering, but Edmond doesn't see them.

15
THE BELLIER-BEAUMONTS
From Burgundy to Sainte-Suzanne,
17th-19th century

They suddenly felt a passion for wild, windswept lands, shores streaming with sugar, the abundance of this white gold. It was decided. They would set sail for this island that was still but a dot to the South on a portolano chart.

Ferréol's story begins on the steps of a house in Burgundy, where his great-grandfather is fastening his traveling bags. At that time, most of his neighbors worked on tenured land that would never belong to them, prayed to a god who didn't hear them, died, usually, when their thatched cottage went up in flames, or its stone walls collapsed. But the young Martin Joseph Bellier leaves the town of Tonnerre for Paris, where the prospects seem better to him. We see him sailing down the river Armançon in a small boat, crossing the Vallée du Serein, boarding a stagecoach, hurtling down dirt tracks, climbing hills planted with elms, riding past fields of turnips, muddy roads, villages with elongated dwellings. The hours go by, then the days, and still the stagecoach carrying Martin Joseph trundles through large forests, close to wide rivers, and in thick fogs that allow only the sound of the hooves and whinnying of the tired horses to be heard. We lose sight of him, imagine he's been robbed by highwaymen, gotten lost, or died in one of the many accidents that are a daily feature of French transport. When we find him again by chance, far away, very far away from his native Yonne and the fresh morning on which he left it, five years have gone by and Martin Joseph Bellier, more dashing than ever, is seated behind an oak desk, wearing the red-sleeved gown of the aldermen of Paris. Other weeks, other months, other years go by. Bellier walks through the dark, damp, and narrow streets of Paris, takes three livres out of his leather purse, and settles inside a four-horse coach leaving for Versailles. It pours with rain for the entire journey. Soaked to the skin, Martin Joseph arrives in front of the great royal gate and promises himself that he will pass through it. Other weeks, other months, other years go by. The sun returns, Martin Joseph does, too. But when he reappears, Martin Joseph is on the other side of the golden gate, as counsellor to the king.

In the end, this "far away" seems still too close to him. He wonders what lies beyond the Trianon, beyond the Jardin de la Reine, beyond Poitou, beyond the Atlantic, beyond the invisible line of the equator. He passes on this curiosity and longing for adventure to his son, Martin Adrien. At twenty, the latter boards a huge sixty-ton cargo ship, surrounded by those shivering rustics, doleful and dazed, who dream of making their fortune in the tropical heat. Martin Adrien becomes an employee of the Compagnie des Indes.

From the deck of the ship, standing on a metal-hooped trunk, Martin Adrien wishes his father the fortitude to put up with the court intrigues, the sullenness of the Parisians, the afternoon downpours, the squeaking of the rats at the Sunday poultry market. He bids him farewell with a feeble wave, lips quivering, as the mainsail is hoisted up.

The ship sets off; it sails through the days, through the nights, under clear skies, towards the endless horizon. Far, very far from the perpetual grayness, the strolls on the Pont-Neuf, the graves of *grand-papa* and *grand-maman*. The passengers don't look backwards, avoid the stern, never regret. On Martin Adrien's lips, but two words, with no verb: far away. No past, no today. Only tomorrow, far away.

"Far away," for Ferréol's grandfather, means the island of Bourbon. Because there the water is drinkable, the terrain vast, with barely a thousand inhabitants. After three months at sea, early one morning, Martin Adrien disembarks at Saint-Paul. He crosses the town swaying like a drunkard, the roiling of the ocean still in his ears. He walks to the church to consult the only available map of the various parishes. Once in front of it, Martin Adrien turns stiff as a post. Nothing but male saints' names: Saint-Paul, Saint-Denis, Saint-Leu, Saint-André, Saint-Benoît, Saint-Pierre. He searches, hesitates, scratches the nape of his neck, mutters. Suddenly, he points at an inkblot on the edge of the main road between Saint-Denis and Saint-Benoît. Finally, a female saint!

"Sainte-Suzanne," he says out loud, as if baptizing the town himself.

No sooner shouted than adopted. Armed with his luggage, his skin still covered in sea spray, Martin Adrien decides to settle in Sainte-Suzanne, a village of ten houses, ten dogs, ten guns. In his newly acquired cart, pulled by two zebus, he has a bowl, three hens, and a rooster attached with string. And that's how he discovers Bourbon, from its lower slopes to the top of its peaks, a succession of forests opening onto mountains, three leagues from the coast, at the end of the world. Bumping along over large stones, Martin Adrien's cart—that is, a patchwork of boards lashed together with liana and rope—advances with difficulty. Saint-Paul to Sainte-Suzanne, twelve leagues, fifty kilometers that take him five-and-a-half days to cover, without encountering a soul, apart from a Creole, twelve slaves, a few Chinamen from Singapore, and two flamingos.

The first Belliers on Bourbon favored the east of the colony, where the soil was moist, the yields better, life not yet grim.

It was then the 18th century, an almost golden period when the land belonged to the first person to settle on it. A colonist would stick a picket into the ground, shout at the top of his voice, "This is mine!", and "this", that's to say, countless

hectares, became his. On condition that the new owner cultivated those hectares with the blessing of the Compagnie des
Indes.

The Bellier in the tropics would remember his father's direc-
tive to go always further. He became the king's commissioner.
Thanks to wanting to go even further, he worked his way up
to running the colony. It was then 1767. On March 31, Martin
Adrien Bellier was officially declared Governor of Bourbon.
The land all around him was still worthless; a hectare would
be exchanged for an old horse or a small gun. At thirty-six, his
wife Marianne bit hard on a piece of wood and brought a little
boy into the world who was named Ferréol Marie Bellier de
Beaumont. And that Ferréol, created during Bourbon's dark
nights, was the father of our Ferréol.

1786. Sainte-Suzanne was fifty-men strong and Ferréol
Marie Bellier de Beaumont twenty-seven years old when he
married Marguerite Dejean. Their descendants started their
own families, married Lepervanches, cultivated the land,
were in politics. To distinguish their lineage, the children and
grandchildren would be given the first name of their father
or grandfather; to stir things up, malicious gossips would say
they'd had a few mistresses. Weary of this controversy over
names and rumors of adultery, they just focused on their ca-
reers, wanting them to be solid as rock. They replaced the
work their ancestors once did with labor that slaves would
now do for them.

Certain colonists would go further to establish their wealth
and prestige. Despite their Madagascan blood, some would
claim to be thoroughbred aristocrats; others followed the fashion for nobiliary particles; still others gradually moved from being mere growers to embracing botany and rare plants. More
classy, more noble, less bumpkin! They could be heard from
afar. A new cutting, an unknown flower? Hands off! It's ours!

Aside from all those types, there was Ferréol. He had the choice between being a truck farmer-florist, a merchant-gardener, a doctor-apothecary, or a politician-nurseryman. He became a landowner-botanist. He would see a potential nursery in every plot of land, stick marigolds into the buttonholes of his hunting jackets, and turn any gun into a support for his tomatoes.

16
THE SPREADING OF THE NEWS
Bourbon, 1842

*"And that's how, from the start, news of the interesting
discovery rapidly spread across our little island."*
—Letter from Ferréol Bellier-Beaumont
to Eugène Volcy-Focard, 1862[15]

T he secret to hand-pollinating vanilla flowers has been
discovered at Ferréol Beaumont's. The secret of the rarest fruit has been discovered at Ferréol's."
It's November 1842, the time of year when vanilla reaches
maturity, and across Sainte-Suzanne, this is all Edmond now
hears about.

The news leaves the Bellevue neighborhood, passes from
aristocratic mouth to bourgeois ear, from Creole villa to sugar
factory, and before nightfall, reaches Saint-Pierre twice. The
first time, it takes a stagecoach from Sainte-Suzanne and makes
the bumpy journey directly to the southern town. It travels fast,
down the swift slopes of Sainte-Suzanne, crossing the Grande
Rivière Saint-Jean on horseback, almost leaping from tree to
tree in the Deux-Rives forest, before breathlessly descending
again towards the Quartier-Français. It travels along the lengthy
avenues, past the houses, and stops dead at the place known as
Champ-Borne, because it can't find an available horse to descend further south. The news continues to spread in the east
on the lips of a Mozambican in a blue Pondicherry-cotton shirt.
Like a whirlwind, he crosses the iron bridge slung between the
Mât river's two stony banks, passes on the news in Bras-Panon,
reaches Saint-Benoît in the middle of the night.

The news also races towards Saint-Denis. Before the cathedral bell has even rung midday, amid the humming of the

[15] *Archives de Bourbon no. 10.*

steam engines, at the front of the carts loaded with cane, at the entrance to the mill, the rumor is swirling that a Creole has revealed the secret of the vanilla flower. By the way, what's vanilla? Most Bourbonnais don't know because, as Volcy-Focard states, until 1841, vanilla only grew in the gardens of a few rare-plant enthusiasts.

Who cares! The less it's known about, the more it's talked about!

It is imagined to cure scabies, improve fertility, bring riches and many descendants to all who find it. The news very soon circulates among the slaves, who have a habit of eavesdropping while their masters gossip. The "inventor" is said to be the color of soot, or rather, of ink. At Bellevue, sides are changed. Those who once criticized Edmond now can't praise him enough. A kind of pride takes hold. Edmond is suddenly a paragon, a hero. Edmond? Of course I know him. They puff out their chests. He's a cousin, a nephew, a half-brother. In Commune-Carron, a cobbler claims that he's his son. In Bel-Air, four women who've given birth name their babies Edmond. On Ferréol's estate, a little girl is baptized Vanille. In short, masters and slaves alike are gripped by a jumble of ambiguous, contradictory, changing feelings. One day they want to bask in Edmond's glory, the next they curse him. And the day after that, they're asking again what vanilla is.

For a few weeks, the rare newspapers available make this new discovery their lead story. In *L'Indicateur colonial*, and Bourbon's other weekly papers, in the cool of verandas and the bustle of markets, everyone's talking about the hand-pollination of vanilla. Edmond, a little Creole of barely twelve, has just found this ingenious method for pollinating vanilla flowers, inspired by pumpkins. It's a new spice that is said to be worth far more than coffee, sugar, and even gold. The editor of the *Courrier de Saint-Paul* devotes an entire article to it. The editor of the *Créole*, journalist and poet Eugène Dayot, moves heaven and earth to question Edmond. It's the first time a Cafre has been in the papers for something other than an escape, a trial, a theft, or a revolt. Until 1855, a third of letters exchanged between the bourgeois of Bourbon mention vanilla and a Creole named Edmond. Some claim that he's Black, Cafre, a slave. People struggle to believe it. No, no, no one's ever seen such a thing. Edmond is surely the name of a white Cafre!

1843. Augustin Eugène Desprez, mayor of Sainte-Suzanne, notices a carousel of carriages and poste chaise revolving around Ferréol's house. The horses whinny, set off, slow down, trot past again; a long line of carts drawn by drowsy oxen, there since the previous day, watch them. Curiosity has replaced surprise. Some men stride along the driveway lined with *filaos* and *chocas*.[16] Others walk silently, dripping with sunshine, trampling vast stretches of golden dust. Demonstrations are requested. Some want to borrow this slave prodigy who knows everything about vanilla. Five young, fifteen-year-old Cafres for that little Negro! Two hectares and a manor in Bordeaux. Ferréol wiggles his toes, a sign of satisfaction with him, promises he'll think about it, agrees to a demonstration, just one, in the meantime.

Edmond never expected this vanilla story to become so big, and confer real importance on him, such a minuscule part of the anonymous masses who tread the path of History without ever leaving a trace. He doesn't realize he has become the missing link between the Old World and Sainte-Suzanne. Everyone studiously avoids telling him so. Such concepts are beyond him anyhow, but he instinctively picks up certain truths. Only yesterday, he was ignored. Today he's being treated with unusual respect. Now he only ever travels by carriage or on horseback to visit Monsieur so-and-so, or the Widow such-and-such, to

---

[16] A low-growing plant with long, tough leaves.

explain how it's done. He blushes at the thought that he may have some talent, certainly small as a bee—it could fit on the tip of a thorn on a lemon tree—but talent all the same. The word doesn't come from him, he heard it said one day as he was passing by.

The talk was of vanilla and a slave with talent.

For the first time in their lives, Edmond and Ferréol are dreaming of piasters and écus collected into small, equal piles; of a sign saying Beaumont & Co.; of their names appearing in a History book. Swiftly, a priest arrives and recognizes the miracle: Ferréol, who had been sick for months, is permanently cured of his mysterious affliction.

"Where's my Edmond? Why hasn't he come to see me all this time?"

He now refers to him only as "the black star of Bourbon," and at moments of ineffable affection, *"mon ti gâté l'amour"*— my beloved little darling.

In his dreams at night, Edmond hears Ferréol talking about him to Elvire and Grand-Marron. Edmond, his Edmond, isn't one of those idlers from that hilly Mozambique, where they snore all day under tents full of headrests and tobacco leaves. Edmond, his Edmond, is a peerless slave, alert as a stag, able to speak Latin and think in Greek. No! No! No! He's not a slave like those of the Desbassayns, of which twenty together don't make an apprentice gardener! He's a lover of plants, a real slave with a green thumb! He performs miracles, I tell you! He's a branch of the Banque de France all on his own! He plants pumpkins that grow big as coaches!

17
EDMOND ON TOUR
Côte-au-Vent, 1843

Treated with "care uncommon towards slaves,"[17] he no longer circulated on foot: "a carriage or horse would be sent to him."[18]

September 15, 1843. A truly festive day. The bells of Sainte-Rose's church alert the growers and the crowd of onlookers gathered there since morning, thus for six hours, that the demonstration is about to begin. For a week, facades of houses have been decorated, the main street swept, a banquet table set up under the lychee trees. The entire village now hurries off to a vanilla nursery close to a ravine, in the middle of a dense and muggy forest. A French flag has been planted there. Among the crowd, spread out on both sides of a row of vanilla plants, there's loud yawning and stretching. Half a dozen olive-green creepers, laden with pale-green flowers, wind around the trunks of every guava, *jambrosade*,[19] and palm tree. The wife of a grower crosses the row of support trees, uncovering a tray of roasted pistachios and fondants, while a slave's melancholy singing is interrupted by someone throwing a pebble.

"Spare us those old dying-dog blues! We want one of those *maloyas* you usually deafen us with."

"No. There isn't time. He's here. Get out the inkpot, quill and notebooks!"

The little Black boy they're waiting for has just arrived.

[17] *Archives de Bourbon no. 10*, a letter from Ferréol Bellier-Beaumont to the public prosecutor, undated, 1855.

[18] *Archives de Bourbon no. 10*, a letter from Mézières Lepervanche to the Governor, December 8, 1853.

[19] The rose-apple tree, its fruit having a delicate flavor of rose, water, and lychee.

Edmond, in a cotton shirt and white boater, with bare feet, is ready to give his first lesson on the pollination of vanilla, watched on by an enthusiastic Ferréol. People rush to greet him—good grief, it's true that he's Black—then form a wide guard of honor leading to a vacoa tree, cut to the size of a man, to which a few scentless blooms cling. In all the towns along the Côte-au-Vent—Sainte-Rose, Saint-Benoît, Saint-André, Sainte-Suzanne, Sainte-Marie—Edmond explains, describes, and demonstrates the technique that enables vanilla to be pollinated by hand.

"You grasp the base of the flower between thumb and middle finger. With a little instrument held in the right hand—a splinter of bamboo, a needle, a pin, or a lemon-tree thorn—you tear or lift the operculum, which is in the form of a lid, separating the pistil from the stamen. With this flap removed, the fertilization organs are exposed; you put the female organ, the pistil, into contact with the male organ, the stamen, with the help of the bamboo splinter. All that's left is to gently draw away the splinter; the flower is fertilized. The pod reaches its adult size, around fifteen to twenty-four centimeters, some six to seven weeks after pollination. Nine to ten months later, the pod reaches maturity and may be picked."

At first, all around him, there's the same silence, heads turning, eyes meeting. Is that it? Just that? Then comes a torrent of applause, making all the vanilla flowers tremble, and a few drop off. The landowner yells, the crowd calms down: each flower hides a pod, each pod a gold ingot. Edmond demonstrates it one more time, before leaving for another vanilla nursery. Thank goodness there are only a few of them, he thinks.

In the east, where it rains almost every day, vanilla nurseries develop fast under Edmond's instruction. He's no great teacher, being short on expressions and imagery, and doesn't speak loudly enough, but he's determined and patient. He teaches with his hands more than his words, rushes from one residence to another, one flower to another. Edmond no longer knows whether he's coming or going. One day he's at Monsieur de Floris's place in Saint-André; on another he travels by boat to Saint-Benoît, where Patu de Rosemont awaits him for some hand-pollination; on yet another, he's pollinating the Vinets' flowers in Sainte-Marie; and on a fourth day, he faces four hours of being carried in a chair along the Chemin Crémont, suspended between sky and earth, to pollinate at the Celestins'. The following month, he's received by Antonin Sigoyer, representing the Desbassayns family, in Sainte-Suzanne.

Edmond only ever glimpses Isidore, Colombine, and Grand-Marron from behind the window of the barouche that takes him from one vanilla nursery to another. They watch him like those cows that watch locomotives go by, not imagining that Edmond envies them, that he's not treated much better than those cattle, barely worth milking.

One morning, when Ferréol is exhausted from accompanying Edmond all over Bourbon, he has the idea of offering group training sessions in his own vanilla nursery. Training disciples, who can then train others. That way, Edmond won't waste his time and can continue to pollinate Ferréol's vanilla plants, which produce three to four kilos of green vanilla pods a year. During the four months of flowering, Edmond pollinates at first around twenty flowers a day, then fifty, then two hundred, and as the years go by, up to one thousand five hundred. He doesn't complain, doesn't ask for water, gives one demonstration after another, and, come evening, goes home to his Ferréol, as long as everyone is proud of him.

He has visited most of the towns and villages along the Côteau-Vent, crossed twenty-five ravines, eight stone bridges, dozens of smaller bridges, covered one hundred and twenty-six kilometers between east and west, alternating walking, stagecoach, sailing, cart, and riding on horseback. In any case, he wakes up every morning pleased to have contributed to something or other of which his mother is proud.

18
EXOTIC VANILLA VS COLONIAL VANILLA
Atlantic coast, middle of the 19th century

*In all the major Atlantic towns, from Bordeaux to Lorient,
all anyone's talking about is vanilla-flavored desserts. Vanilla-
flavored mille-feuille, vanilla-flavored macaron, vanilla-flavored
tart, vanilla-flavored shortbread, vanilla-flavored meringue.*

The first time Edmond sinks his teeth into a vanilla pod, he expects the taste of caramel candy, a flavor that's sweet and vivid, seeming to dance on his tongue. He closes his eyes and forgets the world around him: Grand-Marron, with his coal-black skin and pauper's castoffs, who is pruning the bougainvillea bushes with shears; Colombine, who is weaving a wreath of flowers to place on their son's grave; Isidore, habitual killjoy and spoilsport, who says it's all going to end in disaster. Edmond takes a bite, chews, and lets out a shriek that startles the other three.

"*Lé âcre!*"—It's bitter!—he's cries, grimacing.

He's back again, without warning, in that drab world he'd barely left a bite ago. Edmond is so astounded, he staggers back, spitting what he's just chewed out onto the ground: vanilla has no aroma, no taste, except that of the common green bean.

In fact, a good many growers are realizing, like him, that the raw fruit of the vanilla plant is as tasteless and odorless as a glass of tepid water.

The spark from Edmond's discovery lights a long fuse that crosses the cane fields, the coffee plantations, the dirt road of Sainte-Suzanne, the minds of all the vanilla-growers, finally to explode around ten years later in the form of a question in the head of Ernest de Loupy, a grower in Saint-André. What did the Aztecs do to release the flavor and aroma of vanilla?

Unlike Edmond, Loupy can read, so he dives into travel

journals that describe Aztec procedures. He's soon trying out obscure practices that are halfway between the Mexican method and torture by the Spanish Inquisition: he pulls each vanilla pod by the tail, removing it from the bunch, cuts it open with his fingernails, encloses it in a basket, and blanches it. Then he tips out the contents of the soaked basket onto the ground. After a quarter of an hour, he exposes the vanilla pods to the sun for six to eight days. At one fell swoop, the vanilla has aged by twenty years and Loupy feels ten years younger, but that's not the end of it. He shuts all the pods away indoors, on drying racks for months. Next, he takes a length of tough raffia and ties fifty pods together with it, before storing the bundles inside tin boxes, which are then placed in a wooden crate, surrounded by darkness and sawdust.

In his *Notices diverses sur la culture du vanillier, la féconda-tion des fleurs et la préparation de la vanille*,[20] David de Floris confirms Loupy's process: "This basket is plunged for 18 to 20 seconds into a cauldron of hot, but not boiling, water. [. . .] Next, after removing the pods from the basket, they are imme-diately placed onto dried grasses, woven raffia, hessian *gonis* or *saisis*, to drain. Around a quarter of an hour later, they are exposed to the sun for six to eight days [. . .] until they become brown and withered. [. . .] After the desired exposure to the sun, they are placed in the shade in a well-ventilated place, on racks still covered with woolen blankets, in order to hasten the drying process, prevent mold, and, especially, keep the supple-ness demanded by commerce despite being dry. [. . .] It is easy to know when the pods are dry because they turn black, or rather, chocolate-colored. [. . .] The dried pods are selected and placed into tin boxes, where they reach the perfect level of

[20] "Various notes on growing the vanilla plant, pollinating the flowers, and preparing vanilla," by David de Floris, Philibert Voisin, Michély, Mélinon, C. Cassé; Comité central d'exposition, 1874.

desiccation and suppleness." They are then placed in "bundles of fifty pods and tied together in the middle."

It's only at this price—a high one, Edmond suspects—that Bourbon vanilla reaches its full flavor and releases its aroma. Vanilla needs nearly two years to be ready to eat: you must wait a year before picking it; you then prepare and transform the picked pod—scalding, draining, drying, selecting, grading, wrapping—for another entire year.

Edmond can't get over being the cause of all this processing of vanilla, having finally uncovered its secret. He's proud to be the first link in this long chain of transformation. It'll make another great story to tell his future grandchildren. If one day he has some.

For the moment, Edmond is but an inventor without a patent, thanks to whom the island of Bourbon becomes the first producer of the rarest fruit in the whole world. In 1848, the island that has been renamed La Réunion exports a few dozen kilos of vanilla, which becomes two hundred kilos at the beginning of the 1850s, three tons in 1858, two hundred tons in 1898. By the end of the 19th century, vanilla is as profitable as sugar. It even bags the top prize at the World Fair of 1867. Some four thousand hectares—or eight thousand four hundred soccer pitches—are planted with vanilla.

The flavor sweeps across Europe, it's a new spice that all merchants, bourgeois, gourmets, cooks, and apothecaries are desperate to get hold of.

Overnight, from the main Atlantic ports such as Nantes, Bordeaux, and Le Havre, vanilla is transported upriver in large boats covered in casks. Tumbling from the decks, buckling on the banks, zigzagging through the maze of narrow streets between stalls, pedestrians, and roving fruit- and vegetable-sellers, the sacks of sugar, crates of vanilla, and casks of rum invade every corner of towns in which fortunes are spent on food.

In all the capitals of Europe, small cafés open where patrons gather in front of a cup of raven-black sludge they call hot chocolate *à la vanille* or coffee *à la vanille*. On the dirt tracks leading to town centers, grocers driving barouches offer a black pod, fifteen to twenty-four centimeters long, promising it's a golden investment for the tastebuds. In Paris, they add Edmond's vanilla pod to meringue; in Geneva to milk; in London to pudding; in Palermo to oil; in India to tea; in Bourbon to rum; in Martinique to sugar; in Syria to nougat; in Spain to the creamy San Marcos cake; and in Lisbon to the little tarts everyone calls *pastéis de nata*.

Now, on dessert plates in grand hotels, no one can do without vanilla. All sweet dishes seem to be covered in freckles, tiny black dots like the eyes of ants, staring up at starving gourmets. On store windows, from Nantes to Bordeaux, to the word "sugar" is added the new selling point: vanilla. Here, *brioche à la vanille*, there *crème brûlée à la vanille*, next door, vanilla ice cream, nearby, vanilla cookies, steps away, *madeleines à la vanille*, right beside a vanilla-flavored custard tart, *crêpes à la vanille*, and a vanilla cake. All to be enjoyed with tea infused with . . . vanilla.

Women even go so far as to make eyeshadows with the black vanilla seeds, or freckle their faces with them. In the evening, they wash their bodies with vanilla soap, in marble bath tubs to which the vanilla seeds stick.

As for perfumers, in a France where, from dawn to dusk, the streets are littered with animal carcasses, vegetable peelings, tubercular spittle, and beggars' excrement, they abandon the traditional scents of violet, lavender, and patchouli, instead praising to the skies the new fragrance in its glass phials labeled *Piton noir*, *Île-vanille*, *Bourbon noir*, or *Bleu archipel*. And even then, those are but scents for the trysts of women weavers and vinegar-distilling men!

On the rue de Rivoli, a perfumer creates *Sud sauvage*,

of which dandies and court ladies can't get enough. Across high-society Paris, there's talk of its bluish, sweet, smoky, and also animal notes. A world apart from all the familiar scents. Across high-society Paris, there's praise for this vanilla-bergamot-basil perfume presented in a crystal bottle tied with ribbon and nestled in satin. It's out of this world, this *Sud sauvage.* A magical perfume has been created, sensual as a frisson.

In the other hemisphere, Edmond is unaware that a centuries-old rivalry between the pâtissiers of Nantes and Bordeaux is raging and they're at daggers drawn. Besides the choux buns *à la vanille*, eclairs *à la vanille*, and blancmange *à la vanille*, it's a race to see who, on the Atlantic coast, will create the most original, delicious, unforgettable vanilla-enhanced dessert, according to these gentlemen's discerning palates.

Edmond knows nothing of the *gâteau nantais à la vanille*, that moist little pound cake, round and wide as the palm of a hand, that sells in its hundreds every day between the rue Boileau and the Passage Pommeraye. Edmond doesn't know that an ambassador from the King of Spain, visiting the Bouffay neighborhood, let out a fierce "*¡Ay, caramba!*" when he first tasted the *gâteau nantais* flavored with rum and vanilla.

Edmond rises in the morning not knowing that, for centuries, the *cannelé de Bordeaux* will owe all its vanilla and sugar to Sainte-Suzanne. Edmond lunches unaware that everywhere, from the banks of the Erdre to the Garonne, a cavalcade of merchants, pâtissiers, growers, and perfumers are making a fortune. Edmond has supper oblivious that in the Marais neighborhood, a grocery store called "Chez Edmond" is selling vanilla-based products for eye-watering prices. Edmond falls asleep not suspecting that the politician Léon Gambetta is crazy about *pain perdu à la vanille*, and endlessly repeats, at intimate gatherings: "Vanilla, always eat it, never forgo it."

After France, vanilla sets off to conquer the entire planet.

Across the world, there's a whiff of vanilla in the air; the pods circulate, are sold, bought, consumed without anyone knowing that a twelve-year-old slave, who has never seen a planisphere, had unlocked the secret for the centuries to come, and all with a mere flick of the hand. Edmond doesn't yet know that, for thirty-nine years, on both sides of the equator, people will grow rich thanks to his fingers, and on his back.

The only thing he does know is that in Bourbon, where they prefer savory dishes in a sauce to desserts, a cook from Bordeaux, having arrived on the island with four ducks, and wanting to fit in immediately, decided to combine fowl and vanilla, thus making the very first *canard à la vanille* in history, a dish that remains a great specialty of the island to this day. Edmond has heard of it, but never tasted it.

19
MONSIEUR BEAUMONT
The pinnacle, middle of the 19th century

La vanille, c'est moi!

Ever since Edmond started explaining to anyone interested how to pollinate vanilla, the orchid has ceased to belong to him, for good. On the east coast of Bourbon, the vanilla plantations are multiplying. From the first flowering, they become vast open-air brothels where droves of hired workers serve as go-betweens, titillating the pistil, tickling the stamen, pollinating up to two thousand flowers every day. The success is such that a nickname is found for these pollinators of vanilla. Now, across the island, they're called *"les marieuses"* — the matchmakers.

From the 1850s onwards, all the *vanillards*, as growers of the orchid are known, widen their network of friends, present wedding dresses to their daughters. Without asking those daughters their opinion, they make them marry the sons of prominent local families. Increasingly, on invitations, a certain vanilla grower will no longer scruple to write that *he's* uniting by marriage with Monsieur Borghese or Monsieur de Simplice. The two future fathers-in-law walk side by side in the church, cigar in hand, snuffbox in pocket. To the priest's question they reply in unison, "I do," forgetting the bride and groom. Come dessert, it's *choux à la vanille* for everyone! For a father-in-law to see his matrimonial strategy through, he needs other rich landowners, industrialists, politicians, then senior officials, and finally bank managers. Just one more wedding and he'll be a millionaire. He'll have to consider making his daughters divorce, or poisoning a few sons-in-law, if he's to achieve his ends swiftly. He believes in unhappiness; his happiness depends on it.

Soon, the family reunions of the vanilla planters and biggest sugar producers in the east look more like board of directors' meetings at which *monsieur* speaks of his plans, of his new still, of the imminent departure of his son—Antoine, Hilaire, or Boniface, he's not sure now, he's always mixed them up—for Paris, where he'll receive a proper education. As for the youngest one, who's too effeminate for his liking, he hopes to make a monk or priest of him.

In Bellevue, Ferréol's address book is filling up more than his wallet, but the rumors are increasing. It's whispered that his name has been put forward for the next bestowing of the Légion d'honneur. On Monday, he's thought to be a member of Opus Dei. On Tuesday, a detective claims he's keen on alchemy. On Wednesday, he's said to be the éminence grise of the Governor. On Thursday, they think he's a Franc-Créole, a local type of freemason. He now only travels in a barouche with curtained windows, flanked by two other carriages with equally dark windows. He's said to belong to literary societies, to write poems on the love affair between a pistachio tree and an umbrella fern; everyone applauds, no one laughs.

"Come now, it's Monsieur de Beaumont! The man at whose place vanilla was discovered."

His life is a fantasy, just as, once, it could have been a tragedy.

Indeed, a duel of secret fantasies has begun between Edmond and Ferréol. In his grandest dreams, Edmond sees himself as a partner and peer of Ferréol. First, he'll be emancipated, then he'll buy two hectares, which he'll plant with vanilla, medlar and mango trees, and longan bushes. Next, together they will run a huge company, La Vanillière des Mascareignes—the vanilla producer of the Mascarene Islands. With a bit of luck, one of them will obtain the post of general secretary to the corporation of vanilla growers, while the other will be a town-council man. Suddenly, without them knowing it, their thoughts meet: which of them for the position of Governor? And who will water the orchids?

In one of the dreams he has at night, while shouting, "Yes, yes!" Edmond attends the inauguration of the future lighthouse of Sainte-Suzanne, which naturally bears his name.

Sometimes, when he rises, Ferréol wonders what would have become of him had he not taken in Edmond.

Edmond, his Edmond, had a genius idea that has made all the vanilla growers on the island notably richer. Thanks to his Edmond, vanilla is now a product known to everyone. He shouts at the top of his voice: my teaching, my estate, my advice. He repeats left, right, and center, my Edmond, my slave, my orchid. Standing at the lectern and giving his speech upon being appointed to the Légion d'honneur—you never know—with Edmond silently by his side, Ferréol sees, through the window, the cargo of pods heading for the quay at Saint-Denis and the stores of France, safe in their tin boxes. His eyes light up like beacons, his forehead smooths out. In front of Edmond, who almost chokes as if something has gone down the wrong way, Ferréol exclaims, loud and clear:

"*La vanille, c'est moi!*"—I *am* vanilla!

20
EDMOND AND ICARUS
High, very high

There was once an exceptional, curious, ambitious young man driven mad by studying the humanities, the daily dose of mathematics, and Ancient Greek.

P*ar comment, la vanille c'est li?*"[21]
Edmond would like to stick up for himself, have the words to write to the Governor, to those Gros Blancs of Saint-Denis, and tell them that, actually, *he* is vanilla. Failing that, he'd like to thrash all the *vanillards*, after first chopping off their fingers and spraying chili-pepper juice into the eyes. In one of his rages, as dark as his thoughts, Edmond spurns vanilla as a rotten fruit, a spoilt fruit, maggoty, over-ripe, poisonous.

He imagines running away with Grand-Marron and Colombine to somewhere in the Mafate Cirque, or the Grand Brûlé, hoping to find a cave, a tree at the foot of which he would lie like the dogs when sleeping outdoors. He may only have the dignity of a young slave, that's to say no dignity at all, may not grasp the magnitude of all that's going on behind his back, but he senses that he's the victim of a massive swindle. The gold mine that is vanilla in exchange for a pony ride and a milk sorbet, that's hardly a good deal.

Since Edmond is only fourteen, and isn't sure he'd survive more than a day in vast forests, tracked down by slave-hunters, he settles for pulling grotesque faces and aiming silent insults at Ferréol behind his back, while he rakes the garden.

Edmond tells himself that if he went to school, if he was attending Brother Scubilion's school for Blacks, he'd never

---

[21] "What does he mean, he *is* vanilla?"

THE RAREST FRUIT · 119

have been had like this. He'd start court proceedings, ask that Bourbon vanilla be named after him:

"*Vanilla borbonica edmundii.* Hell that sounds good!"

But then, school seriously terrifies him, because he knows very well that it may have no effect on Whites, but it makes Blacks go mad. The masters say so, and Edmond's convinced it's true. Indeed, they've all been telling their slaves the same story for a hundred and fifty years.

The story is that of a young man of mixed race, an exceptional, curious, ambitious, courteous young man, kind to slaves, driven mad by studying, the humanities, and the daily dose of mathematics. One need go no further than Sainte-Suzanne to find just such a young man, whom everyone already saw as a physicist, an astronomer, or the Governor. For sure, he would become one of those heroes who rouse an entire nation, transform science with an apple, observe fifteen new planets through a telescope made one Sunday in May, between Mass and siesta. But none of that happened.

Intelligence had killed him.

One evening, he had gone to bed after a few Latin declensions, a little algebra. In the morning, he had got up and everything had just disappeared. His lucidity, first, then his tutors, and then all the hope that had been pinned on him. Some claim that, having received a letter from the great physicist Volta inviting him, in person, to join him, he went instantly mad with shock. As if thunderstruck. Others say that, from then on, he would talk to himself and succumb to horrifying epileptic fits the moment he conjugated the auxiliary verb *être*. Whatever the case, at sixteen, all that remained to him of the sciences were the parallel lines of the paths that, zombielike, he would pace endlessly up and down. A veritable sentry on a rampart. In the end, he did actually hurl himself from the top of a rampart, got up unscathed, no longer shouted that one plus one equals three, and became the first inhabitant of Bourbon to wear a straitjacket. Because neuroleptics had yet to be invented. Because this straitjacket had to be of use to someone. Whatever the why, the moral of the story endured throughout the century. It reached Edmond: it's better to live dumb and poor than epileptic and nuts.

This tale of ruination is known across the island, appalling all the Blacks, repeated even by their parents. A story that makes none of them want to leave their substratum life. In every drunkard, every loony, every convict, Edmond, like the others, sees the same warning sign: grammar killed me. It kills dead any temptation to write with style. Edmond often thinks about that mixed-race Hercules, humble and generous, with the build of an athlete, the modesty of a priest, the rhetoric of a politician. A catalogue of virtues reduced to bed-wetting, simply for having opened a book. Isidore even gives names, indicates addresses, knows relatives, sometimes a sister. Nothing to do with lurid mythology, this is real life. Edmond realizes that there are more of them than suspected. At least one black Icarus per town, brain burnt by education, for wanting to rise high, too high in the pursuit of knowledge. It's for this reason that Edmond—on the sound advice of Ferréol, who sees no use in him going to school—has always preferred the dining table to tables of contents and multiplication. Has always put belly before head.

21
NO NO NO
The slaves' hut, 1843-1848

Sic vos non vobis, laboratis, servi.
And so you work, slaves, but it isn't for yourselves.

As the years go by, rumors of abolition become as much a part of Edmond's daily life on the estate as the sugarcane. At first, the rumor arrived like the echoes of a distant war punctuated by colossal defeats. In hushed voices, the masters would pass the news on to each other and write down, in little notebooks with a clasp, the names of the countries where abolition had won the day. Edmond couldn't place them on the map, he discovered their existence at the same time as their downfall. Denmark had fallen, Haiti, England. Then Peru, Chile, Costa Rica. And even later, Jamaica and South Africa. Same tragedy in Mauritius.

Freedom is something Edmond only has a hazy idea about because, in his family, no one has known it. It's even the only thing, along with happiness, they've never seen. Sometimes he tells himself that, if things become unbearable, he'll kill himself, slowly but surely, by eating soil. Failing that, he'll take Isidore over to some vanilla creepers, plait them like a rope, then beg him to strangle him with it. Knowing Isidore, he won't need to ask him twice.

For now, Edmond has barrowloads of stones and bales of straw to shift, orchids to take cuttings of, weeds to pull, manure to spread. If he gets it right, in the short term, it'll take him until the glimmers of dusk, when you can start to see the Moon clearly. Talking of the Moon, Edmond wonders how it intends for him to come out on top of the situation. Time passes. Edmond is fifteen, it's already 1844!

On March 18, 1844, Ferréol draws up an inventory of his assets. On his Bellevue estate, he owns a great many slaves, young well-built Cafres, Negresses with pert breasts. And not a single old man with droopy testicles, or Negro with withered thighs. One horse, three pigs. And Edmond, ah yes, Edmond, a slave aged around fifteen.

Considering that he's served his master well, Edmond plucks up courage on a day when Ferréol is in a cheery mood, and goes to ask him some questions. He knows that particularly deserving slaves are rewarded with emancipation. At fifteen, he wants to be free.

"Sorry? Say that again?"

"Emancipate me," Edmond requests, already apologizing.

Edmond will never know what he would have done with his freedom because he isn't emancipated. The names of the newly free regularly reverberate around Sainte-Suzanne, but the archives never mention Edmond's name.

On February 28, 1842, Clotilde Anicette, a Creole seamstress, and her son Alexis, who's a year younger than Edmond, both obedient, really obedient, are emancipated in Sainte-Suzanne. On January 28, 1843, everyone surrounds the Indian, Mercure Alexan, a *Noir de pioche*, who works badly, very slowly, who denies having poisoned his three children and two of the farm's cows; his master is freeing him. At the start of 1844, Hamilcar, a semi-alcoholic accused of arson, assault and battery, and false accounting, but not all on the same day—he only has two arms—but all in that same year, 1843, is appointed slave driver. February 5, 1845, Olive Thomy, sixteen, a servant of no great merit, stupid rather than wicked, is emancipated. 1846, Alphonse, always involved in any revolts, was a fugitive for two weeks, claiming he got stuck down a ravine, wants to create an association to defend Blacks' rights, is promoted to commander of slaves. In March 1847, Barnabé Regord, slave laborer, fifty-five, which is ancient at that time, a Creole who is forever complaining of pains, eats like three horses, has a back so lacerated it's hard to know where to apply the riding-crop, is emancipated. On April 14, 1847, Edmond hugs Uranie Brun, twenty years of keeping her head down, of submission, washing, scouring, who now, to her label of Creole is adding that of emancipated. Edmond congratulates a whole crowd of slaves— meek and exemplary, useless or difficult, informers of revolts or instigators—whom their masters are rewarding, releasing, emancipating, or promoting, left, right and center.

Edmond, a slave with talent, remains increasingly alone in front of the huge garden, which all his friends gradually leave, even Bibi, the last, or rather the first of the drunkards. Edmond is seventeen and living surrounded by orchids suddenly demands a superhuman effort of him.

1842-1848, the beginning of a life in which his disappointment is as huge as the basin of Bourbon's Cascade Niagara. Edmond is a doomed bird in a cage to which the master keeps the key.

On November 22, 1848, there's not much joie de vivre left on the Beaumont estate when Ferréol has Edmond's certificate of emancipation brought over to him. In the garden, Edmond is watering some huge *songe* leaves, also known as elephant ear, down which the water is slowly sliding. He doesn't look up, it's a matter of pride, doesn't take the certificate straight away. In any case, in a few days' time there'll be no more slaves in Bourbon. With faith in the legacy of his earlier discovery, Edmond hopes to use it to begin a new life. Edmond is a leaf, and leaves don't harbor resentment. They wait, come loose, and then fly away when their time comes.

22
THE GREAT NAMES CHARADE
Town hall of Sainte-Suzanne, November 22, 1848

*The citizen Edmond, son of the late Pamphile and Mélise,
did indeed present himself at the town hall, this Wednesday
November 22, to receive a name.*

November 1848, early afternoon. Kicking up a big fuss, Edmond leaves Bellevue for the town hall of Sainte-Suzanne. He has an appointment with a registrar.

To distinguish his new life, in every respect the same as his previous one, he, too, must take a surname, since only real men have them. He's nineteen and tries to convince himself that behind this dive into administrative waters lies a rebirth as safe and reliable as a lifebelt. He feels old and heavy, weighed down with twenty years and twenty kilos of disillusionment, but he still wants to believe that. Up until then, hope has been of no use to him, but he tells himself that a new name, like a baptism, a conversion, will make a different man of him.

For a week, Edmond tries to find a surname he can add to his name. He says hundreds out loud. He thinks of the republican calendar, of the town he was born in; he dives into memories of the water he grew up around—Grande Rivière Saint-Jean and Bassin Racine, Sainte-Suzanne's river and Bassin Canne, Ravine des Chevres and Bassin Boeuf. Edmond Laravine? Edmond Rivière? Names that smell of eels and damp. Brr, he goes, grimacing.

At this time, boys are given names such as Eustache, Philibert, Émile or Jean-Baptiste, names with a whiff of administrative ink, bourgeois drawing rooms, tranquil afternoons beside lily ponds, sipping herbal tea. The last time Edmond drank some of that tea, the herbs stuck to his gullet like leeches; he had to down four liters of water to get rid of them. So, no to all such names. Edmond keeps searching.

After a week, he's narrowed it down to two or three criteria. Nothing that warbles like a blackbird. He wants a name that snaps. A provocation, a slap in the face, a snub to all the Gros Blancs. A name that might precede that of Beaumont, alphabetically. Beginning with the letter A, then. So that if, one day, an *Almanach des Honnêtes Gens* were published, he would feature in a prime position.

A Latin ring to it wouldn't be bad. For all those Latin plant names his head has been stuffed with since he was four. For Linnaeus too, and all their discoveries, and all their petal-strewn adventures. And for the *Vanilla planifolia*, naturally.

As with all moments of extreme tension, when a decision is a commitment for life, when the universe holds its breath, when the slightest mistake would follow you like a ball and chain, Edmond sweats buckets imagining the wrong name attached to his ankles and having to drag it through the jeering for the rest of time. Edmond breathlessly searches for a tribute-name, a thank-you-name, a history-name, a name that will be great, or not at all!

He must also admit: all that's associated with success, with wealth, is white. The Governor, the priest, the members of the Compagnie des Indes, political power, religious influence, they're all grafted onto a pyramid of colors, beneath which the Cafre lies ten feet under, in the sand. To succeed, you have to live white, think white, be White, have a white name.

His name must scream that color.

Outside the town hall, a long line of newly free folks wait to be civilly "baptized." When Edmond's turn comes, the officer Périer-Montbel, a short man with broad shoulders, asks him his first name.

"Edmond."

"Name of last master? And last occupation?"

"*Mon l'ancien maît', c'est missié Ferréol Bellier-Beaumont. Ma la decouv' comment féconde la vanille.*"[22]

"That's not an occupation, is it! And the vanilla you mention, is that the new spice that's finally given some flavor to rice pudding?"

"*Oui, sa même. Par contre . . .*"[23]

Behind Edmond, the crowd is growing impatient. Hundreds of former slaves come and go, greet each other, hug each other, like a column of ants scurrying along a table on which there's a sugar cube. It's a very fine day. From the town hall you can see the sea. They're all keen to get this done.

"Who's taking forever in front? Ten years to pick a name! Faster! Faster!"

By stamping their feet on the checkered paving, they make the dust and the policeman's kepi shudder. Get a move on! Get a move on! Fines for disturbing public order are in the offing, the town-hall officials are panicking. Insults are flying. A mass brawl breaks out. The bird-name slurs come thick and fast: you insolent *papangue*, lazy dodo, vain *tuit-tuit*, chattering mynah, silly *tec-tec*, cheeky blackbird, spouting sparrow!

Up at the front, Edmond is still taking forever.

All this racket makes him forget what he wants to say. It's that man there who's to blame!

"*Kisa? A moin? Ou connaît kisa mi lé?*"[24]

"So you've lost your memory, too!"

Out of this mayhem of words, fists, and impatience emerges the name Albius. Get out! Latin. Who cares! Albius, the

---

[22] "My former master is Monsieur Ferréol Bellier-Beaumont. And I discovered how to pollinate vanilla."

[23] "Yes, the very same. But then . . . "

[24] "Who's that? Me? D'you know who I am?"

comparative. Still this Black fellow? Albius. Whiter. Than whom, than what? Throw him out of here, dammit! Albius. Whiter than the other Blacks, but still too black for all the Whites. Albius like alabaster. Whiter than the White himself. Still this nonsense! Let's go with Albius! The official gives in. And now, get lost.

He can always say it was the choice, or the fault, of this official, who must have learnt Latin, though God knows where. People might think it was Ferréol who chose this patronymic, as singular and unexpected as his first name, Edmond. Who cares! Ignoring the shouting, the eddy of bodies caught up in the brawl, Edmond crosses the foyer of the town hall unscathed and joins the procession of the newly baptized.

A new day dawns. Edmond has a name!

From now on, he is Albius. Edmond Albius.

23
EDMOND AND SARDA GARRIGA
Place du Gouvernement, known as Place du Barachois
December 20, 1848

Free, did you say free?

When December 20, 1848, arrives, the day on which slavery was abolished, Edmond has what optimism remains after nineteen years of sweat and servitude. He is going to leave Ferréol. His heels, tough as a *bardeau*,[25] barely touch the stony ground that leads towards Saint-Denis. His heart is pounding in anticipation of the energetic beating of the drum on the Place du Gouvernement. He leads the way, followed by thousands of marching bare feet. It's a procession of a thousand soles, rough and cracked as bark, flying over the black dust towards a certain Sarda Garriga, emissary of a repentant Second Republic that, all things considered, deems slavery to be inhuman and outdated because it's just too costly.

At first, the masters had balked at declaring their slaves free; one grows attached to those big silly fools. Then, whipped up, they had formed the Assemblée des Propriétaires, evoking a mishmash of the Old Testament and the Curse of Ham. It's not us, it's the others! Next, they had spoken of the far bloodier danger, from tigers, lions, panthers, these miserable lives had been exposed to in the African bush. And not even a word of thanks! To conclude, they spoke of divine will, of the karma of peoples. Who would oppose God, who had created them woodcutters and water-carriers, field workers and rice planters? One cattle breeder shouted louder than the rest. They talk

---

[25] A small tile made of wood or shingle, used to clad roofs and facades of creole houses.

of replacing my draft horses with a steam locomotive, my Moka cattle with a stage coach. And now they want to abolish slavery! I could eat the horses and cattle, but what on earth could I do with the Blacks? Surely you don't want . . . And how they all laughed at this tasteless joke. Then an economist had, as usual, sworn that servitude was the noblest financial and social model a colony could dream of, that any change would be cataclysmic, that the Negroes would die of grief and nostalgia. In the end, they had negotiated seven hundred and thirty-three francs for every Negro lost, and merely swapped the frizzy-haired for the cargo boats of immigrants arriving from India in groups of a hundred. They can take their damned freedom!

In front of the government building, the French flag cracks instead of the whip. Under the lofty palms, a few potbellied officials strut around on horseback or on foot. Between them and the others, there's a line-up of bayonets, police officers, gendarmes, and cannons. The others are the euphoric Africans and Madagascans, the Indians with buns, the Chinese with long plaits. While each different clan awaits the Commissaire Général de la République, Sarda Garriga, and the speech of the century, their expectations are very similar: he'll surely be a White of around a meter ninety, with cocked hat and sword, a Roman nose, a puffed-out chest under a uniform decked in gold with stiff epaulettes and the Légion d'honneur. The crowd surges, the applause thunders when a man of, at most, a meter sixty turns up. The faded *tricolore* sash and rose in the buttonhole are just about acceptable, as is the black jacket with long tails. But the felt hat, out of fashion since winter 1823, shocks the seething crowd. And that's the first of a long series of let-downs. In the middle of this brotherhood of fortune, Edmond turns his disappointed, but still hopeful, eyes to Sarda's scarlet lips, as he shouts something like this:

"France, your country, sends me! France, your mother, blesses you." France this, the Republic that. "The world is changing, my friends!"

There follows an interminable description of an almost epileptic world, starting from the democracy of Athens and the Roman republic, and including emancipations, the vagaries of citizenship, Saint Louis's sessile oak, the humanism of the Republicans. Everyone is dozing off at the foot of the dais when Sarda, after taking a deep breath, bellows the crucial bit:

"France sets you free! She saves you! She no longer has slaves, only citizens. God wills it, the State does it!"

And so, in the midst of the cheers and floods of tears, new words are swirling around. All free. All equal. All brothers. *Zot la fé a nou blanc*—You have turned us all white. The band strikes up "*La Marseillaise*." Instantly, sixty thousand new Whites hold their heads high, grip this new freedom, and cast off their fetters. In the front row, Elvire sheds a tear while saying amen. In Sainte-Suzanne, her brother is drawing up his claim for state compensation for the citizen Albius. The iron shackles burst open, releasing the necks and ankles of the slaves. All around Sarda, some shout out, thank you, others mutter, murderer.

"Long live the Republic! Long live the Colony! Long live the Government!" Sarda cries, fervently.

"Free, did you say free?" Edmond asks.

"Yes, and from now on, unity is what we're after," Sarda replies, going one better.

Communion, junction, combination, juxtaposition, aggregation. Sarda uses all the synonyms of unity he can think of, talks of peoples holding hands, of jigsaw puzzles of lives of which each Black is a piece. Sarda is a one-man Edict of Nantes, a waffler. He speaks of a world-island, of a congregation of religions, and Edmond, without taking it all in, is elated.

There's dancing, a Mass is celebrated. There's hailing of the abolitionist Schoelcher, cursing of Bonaparte. Finally, a huge wave of free men surges past the row of mortars and then parts the guns behind which the estate owners are entrenched in funereal silence.

"Where are they, those Whites? *Où sa zot lé?*—Where have they gotten to? There they are at last! Let's go!"

Under the palm trees, the slaves suddenly fall to their knees before yesterday's torturers; kiss the feet that, only the previous day, would kick in their jaws; smile at the constipated faces that usually crapped on them. Two groups of people are fraternizing out loud who, under their breaths, call each other a filthy race. In the end, the glasses of arack wash away the old grudges from this day that's intoxicated with freedom.

"Let us build an ideal city founded on harmonious coexistence! Let us create a new society without class or king!" The days of fugitives are over, thinks Sarda, getting rather carried away. "All is forgiven, for all of you. The Republic is generous. You were furnishings, and now you are objects. Of respect, of consideration, of love."

Harmonious existence, that's all Sarda ever goes on about, a concept hazy as mist that even he doesn't believe in for a second. At best, it will be a case of together, but separately.

Nearby, Brother Scubilion, who still runs the school for black children, is saying that, somewhere in the Gulf of Guinea, a state by the name of Liberia welcomes emancipated slaves. Colombine and Grand-Marron swear they'll go there. Edmond listens. He doesn't even know where the Mozambique of his ancestors is, so as for Liberia . . .

Edmond firmly believes in freedom, like all the others do. His brain is so damaged that he believes anything, anyhow. Sarda outlines the framework of this new world, built on order and work, a salary and prosperity. Each person will get their due, each will work ten hours every day, and the rest of the time, will be free to do whatever they want, that is to say, nothing.

A semblance is made of burying, beneath an umpteenth *Te Deum* and resounding amen, the yoke of the violence-submission, rage-resignation, docile slave-brutal master dynamic this entire tropical, sun-lashed land is still stuck with today. The chains are melted down, the whips burnt, the ankle bells crushed, the muzzles shredded.

Formerly, this man was an animal. From now on, the animal is a man.

Faced with this metamorphosis, the estate owners can't cope anymore, and so, with pinched expressions and the excuse of a pot on the stove, an orchard to water, their dignity to bury, they all leave, quaking in their boots.

While they are rejoining one of their usual mistresses in the La Montagne neighborhood, back on the Place du Barachois, a soldier fires twelve canon shots, scaring the doves. Only the pigeons remain.

Ten years later, when remembering this day, an emancipated slave, waxing lyrical, declaimed a few lines by a mystical Victor Hugo writing of birds and freedom:

By what right do you put these birds into cages?
By what right do you steal the life from the living?
Beware of somber justice. Beware!
To all who are locked up, give the key to the fields![26]

But for now, a few women are weeping, Edmond is, too; the essential has been said, the journalist concludes. No unhappiness allowed here.

The story continues at Bas de la Rivière.

Where, to the sounds of the *kayamb*, the *banza*, and the *bobre*, the biggest *bal la poussière* Bourbon has ever known is getting underway. A huge open-air dancefloor on which, under a canopy of stars, twirl parasols, flounced dresses, women's shawls, men's arms, old men's hats, priests' bands. All night long, it's an extraordinary medley of Cafres, dancing and song,

[26] Victor Hugo, *La Légende des siècles*, Poésie collection/Gallimard, 2002.

a *kabar*[27] for drum and *rouler*, accompanied by the barking of a little *chien-coton* that just appeared from nowhere, and only stops twice—to drink water from a nearby puddle and chase a cat that's meowing on purpose. Until dawn, the ground shudders under the feet of dancers who are endlessly dispersed and endlessly reunited by glasses of rum that merry Malbars[28] carry on trays above their heads, sweetening the air. They say that, carried by the wind, the singing could be heard as far as Mahébourg, in Mauritius, where the locals laughed heartily at these Réunionnais who, as usual, were thirteen years late in everything: by the time they'd built a road, it would be a dead end; they'd be praying for a lighthouse when Mauritius's Port-Louis would already have a train. And this last remark made some former fugitive slaves, returning from a hunt in that island's Le Morne Brabant, split their sides.

"Here's to the Republic, our grateful cousins!"

In Saint-Denis, they're still swaying their hips, head against head, hands against bodies, begging the night to stand still over the rocky coast. Moon, stop right above Bourbon, and you, Sun, above Basse Vallée! Twelve hours of partying for two centuries of slave trading. Later on, a gendarme would report to Sarda on the damage after the festivities: two old men dying of joy, a Lasallien priest losing his bands, a Madagascan breaking his leg, a baby born close to midnight named Liberté by its mother, and the usual shootout in the Camélias district.

In short, a successful *bal nègre* in the middle of a blazing summer. And that's as far as it all went; they were running towards freedom as if plowing headlong into a wall, Edmond first among them.

---

[27] Celebration with a concert, organized for major events such as the abolition of slavery.

[28] People in La Réunion of South Indian Tamil origin.

24
EDMOND HITS ROCK BOTTOM
The bottom of a hole, 1849-1850

Edmond lives on the bank of a river and the brink of ruin.

Nineteen years old and so many hopes. Edmond bids farewell to Ferréol's garden of orchids and to his rarest fruit. He leaves Sainte-Suzanne and goes up to Saint-Denis, keen to fulfil goodness knows what more or less pious desire. He, too, demands more than his share of ordinary misfortune. He, too, like all those failed by happiness, walks the capital's streets hoping to find gold under the cobbles, open a store, live the life of a prophet, who knows!

At the time, Saint-Denis is a small town in which stores are multiplying. From morning to dusk, men in their thirties, accompanied by stiff and silent wives trussed up in corsets, come and go there, in the midst of a crowd of "new Whites" zigzagging, barefooted, from one job to another. In all of Bourbon's towns, in fact, the Cafres are frenetic, abandoning, like Edmond, their former masters, carrying their belongings on their heads, getting hired by new masters whom they soon quit for barely improved conditions. Doors slamming. Upheaval. Quitting. Rehired, only to pack it in again. The island is a fever that has gripped Edmond. Like all the other freed slaves, Edmond, having taken the first job going so as not to be accused of vagrancy, places an ad in the *Moniteur de l'île Bourbon*:

Cafre, nearly twenty, can't read or write but can count, good gardener, good cook, able to groom horses, make furniture, pollinate vanilla, and ride posthaste, seeks to be a servant in a decent household. Contact Monsieur ***, rue des Mozambiques.

Rue des Mozambiques, that's where Edmond now lives, in a district called Camp des Noirs du Roi. Also sleeping there are the squad of Indians, Africans, Comorans, and Madagascans who form a bloc of sadness in their unfinished huts, then drop like flies after eight, ten years of work. A real refugee camp down by the river. There are no flowers or fruit to pick in Edmond's garden. In fact, there's no garden at all.

Edmond lodges in a hovel with no partitions or solid walls, sparse furniture, and three other Cafres. He lies on a hessian *goni* stuffed with sugarcane straw and sleeps against a window that opens onto a wall of stones. Does Edmond regret having left Ferréol? Is he missed by the man who always called him *mon ti gâté*? We suppose so, but can't be sure. Here again, there's a resounding silence, reminding us that all that we know of their story fits onto just one leaf. Not of paper, that's too big. The leaf of a vanilla plant.

Perhaps, on both sides, there's a touch of male pride, an ounce of jealousy that creates a gulf between them. Perhaps old Ferréol, fifty-seven and childless, curses and laments the departure of a son who grew away from him. Perhaps Edmond no longer calls that love, but rather possession, and that's why he chose the Camp des Noirs, where all is for the best in the worst of worlds; perhaps Edmond doesn't want to see all the efforts Ferréol is making for his lost son. All this remains a mystery. What the archives do say is that a claim for state compensation is addressed to Sarda on Edmond's behalf. What they don't say is whether Edmond received this compensation. It would seem not. Perhaps that letter came too late in Edmond's eyes, and he would have preferred early emancipation to belated écus. It's yet another puzzle that no one can solve.

As far as Edmond was concerned, the Sarda mountain delivered but a mouse dropping.

Each night, knee on floor, hands together, Edmond quietly prays to his God with two faces, Christian and chimakondé, asking him to light up his path and remove his doubts, the questioning. Edmond then does the rounds of the *devinèrs* on the Rue des Guinées. They explain his nightmares, interpret his dreams, endlessly predict an unexpected and remarkable future for him. The universe owes him one. He leaves each sorcerer with lucky charms tied around his waist, bursting with impatience. Everything starts tomorrow, he repeats to himself every morning. Indeed, something is starting that Edmond could never have imagined.

At nineteen years and a few months old, Edmond is coming up against *l'engagisme*, a robust legal construct that goes way back to the *Ancien Régime,* and a longstanding colonial practice, especially common after abolition. In Saint-Denis, he now receives a wage minus food, accommodation, clothing, and medical care. A kind of tropical capitalism where men survive on twelve francs fifty a month, which the colonial elite considers to be too much. Having known only the comfort of Bellevue and the life of a gardener, he now does everything he formerly escaped doing: toiling in fields of cane, corn, clove trees. In quarry, workshop, storehouse. As workman, farmhand, servant.

Edmond works nine-and-a-half hours a day, six days out of seven, with that slight feeling of helplessness of those who are losing, that mix of lethargy, dejection, and despair that psychiatrists would later call post-traumatic stress; romantics would call *la jettatura*, or the curse of the evil eye; and pragmatists would call being stone broke. In short, he discovers the shit life, the habitual oppression of the Blacks, the plight of workhands in the coastal towns. Far from his vanilla plants and Ferréol, Edmond lives on the brink of ruin, on rice, dry vegetables, and a ration of salt. No. He won't return to Ferréol! Yet another shipwrecked life begins, minus Ferréol, plus a rug and two old blankets. He sometimes wants to vomit or die, but immediately decides against it. No, life isn't a hangover. No, life isn't never-ending toothache. No, everything hasn't stayed exactly the same since everything changed. Stubborn as a mule, Edmond clings on to this business of destiny, of vanilla, that governs his life. No, it's not for nothing that he discovered the rarest spice in the world. An unexpected and remarkable future awaits him, it was predicted to him. He will soon be someone and his discovery will serve him well.

25
EDMOND AS COOK
Rue du Four-à-Chaux, Saint-Denis, 1851

*While Edmond awaited trial, the executioner
was paid off and gallows erected.*

Edmond is twenty-two when he starts working as a cook
for Monsieur Marchand, a captain-adjutant residing on
Rue du Four-à-Chaux in Saint-Denis.

He has learnt to cook by hanging around Colombine, who,
from Monday to Sunday, would prepare countless meals at the
end of Ferréol's garden. For years, he helped her to smoke the
marlin and sea urchin, stirring the embers with a stick. Isidore
even reckons that, after orchids, his friend likes smoked goose
most of all. His name is Edmond and he can do everything every which way. Pollinate vanilla and make pumpkin soup and
chicken fricassee.

His luck is starting to turn, leading him towards the unexpected and remarkable happiness he believes he deserves. And
too bad for those birds of ill omen who thought he'd remain
down in the dumps, forever in the dumps.

Marchand, a Chevalier de la Légion d'honneur, with fif-
ty-two years of fine meals under his belt, high up in the colonial
government, knows nothing whatsoever of Colombine or this
vanilla business. In his eyes, Edmond is just one more Black in a
land of seventy thousand of them, maybe one meter sixty-eight
tall, beardless, docile, discreet, a good cook, exactly what he's
after to prepare his family meals and the food for Grouchy, an
eight-month-old poodle whose paws often get under Edmond's
feet. For Edmond, it's a job allowing him to eat his fill in the
home of a Gros Blanc, who's a bit conceited but spares no ex-
pense in the kitchen. Marchand is one of those types who—the

peak of chic and refinement—eat barely any of the produce on which the island's economy and their own fortunes depend. He doesn't like sugar, only drinks aged rum, very rarely coffee, and shuns any dish that's too spicy. Edmond's life is of little interest to him. He needs a cook's boy, not a patented inventor.

So what?

The following Monday, amid the pounding of the pestle, creaking of the cooking pots, bubbling of the sauces simmering on a wood fire at the back of the courtyard, Edmond regains a taste for life through that of the meals he prepares. He makes a tuna curry, vegetable relishes, goose stew, quails stuffed with lychees—dishes that make such a change from his daily pigswill that he says to himself, clicking his tongue: "*Mi en prendrai bien si i rest' in peu.*" I wouldn't mind some if there's any leftover. He hasn't eaten so well since the Bellevue days. Edmond prepares platters of dried fruit, of flower salad, which he serves with fortified wine. He tastes shark fin, prefers chicken stew. Edmond wouldn't say he's happy, but he constantly hears his mother's gentle voice, over and above that of Marchand.

Often, when Marchand is away, Edmond dozes off in his armchair, with his pince-nez on his nose; he dreams he's the owner of this large corniced house, the husband of a rich widow whose fortune he'd squander. He'd dine on roast goose and smoked eel, before going out to greet the Governor, leaning on a pommeled cane. What they'd talk about he never finds out. Every time his dream is disturbed when he hears the creak of the small gate and Marchand's steps. Edmond jumps up, says *b'jour missié*, and returns to his post behind his hot stove.

For weeks, assisted by one of those servants who, when winter colds are rife, blow their nose into the cream desserts, Edmond springs up as soon as Marchand pulls the bell cord; he brings forth pots of crawfish, quails braised with apples, calves' sweetbreads, salt-crusted capon, chicken kidneys, asparagus velouté, young-rabbit filets, which the guests tuck right into while talking business and politics. The months go by, the Marchands get fatter, Edmond's wages shrink. Marchand has had to deduct the fowl he burnt, the Limoges plate he broke, the two slices of tart he ate. Soon, all of his meals are deducted from his wages, and Edmond must pay for his coffee. Next, he's no longer allowed to eat what he cooks. All leftovers are for Grouchy, apart from fish heads, which his little stomach struggles to digest. In the store-room, Marchand counts everything, even the almonds, and weighs the quarters of beef hanging from hooks. In his head, Edmond cries famine. In his heart, he wants his *ti père* Ferréol back.

Edmond is twenty-two and feels tired, with a bitter taste in his mouth. He's tired of living like a *tangue*, digging, digging, and still digging without ever reaching the bottom. Tired of the freedom that chains him up. It's obvious that all his optimism and efforts are futile. He may be breathing, but that doesn't mean he's living.

In his mind, he'd do anything for a few sous and a proper meal: smash bourgeois's doors, slug bread-sellers. He hates himself for not having left with Colombine and Grand-Marron, unaware that their bodies are floating inside a ship that sank a year back.

As he leaves work, he often looks eastward, towards Sainte-Suzanne, but it's not known whether his eyes are burning with rage or regret. His belly contains just greens and fried *chipèks*, the grasshoppers he crunches with a grimace. In the dining room, before the Marchands arrive, Edmond, casual and cavalier, just wants to spit in the squash soup, pick his nose over the gratins, wipe his sweaty brow with the table napkins. In this world of madmen, he's losing both his footing and his mind. And so he considers stealing!

It's the height of August, the vanilla plants are in bloom, a man disappears, taking some swag with him.

No one knows where Edmond is, or what he's up to. Traces of the swag can be found only on August 21, 1851, in the handwriting of a policeman who registers a complaint by an *engagiste*, or post-slavery employer. That *engagiste* is Joseph Mathurin Marchand, Edmond's boss. The complaint is of theft. Marchand has lost a chain, two silver bracelets, a rosewood box containing seashells, and a wallet. Three bottles, a roasted joint, some cheese, and a few items of clothing are also declared stolen.

At first, Marchand suspects an outcast with blond hair, descendant of a long line of mustachioed pirates, who lives close by in a hut full of moths. One of those anarchists exiled to New Caledonia's Kanak bush, who stowed away on a caravel sailing to Bourbon by climbing along a rope between two ships. But then Marchand changes his mind. No outcast, however vile, could do such a thing. All guns turn elsewhere. It's surely a man who knows the house well, the policeman declares on the August 21. You must employ ex-slaves at your place!

"I certainly have one who could be your man!"

As soon as Marchand has left, everyone pictures, and fears, a bloodthirsty Black, bundle on back, knife between teeth, who prowls by night and points his brackmard at any landowner sleeping after a day's work. A Wanted poster is put out:

WANTED DEAD OR ALIVE,
OR ALMOST,
HIGHWAYMAN!

And thus the legend was born of a big, bad, Black thief roaming the dirt tracks between Le Barachois and the Sentier du Cap Bernard. Soon, the name of Edmond Albius is being bandied around. In the Rue du Four-à-Chaux, women and children scatter whenever his name is uttered. From the parvis of the cathedral, a glimpse is caught of a guilty-looking Edmond, perched on an African palaver chair—two interlocking planks, one long and slightly tilted, the other short and horizontal—and planning his next thefts out loud. From the small market to the church, the rumor spreads that the young man who discovered how to pollinate vanilla is an out-and-out chicken thief. Some have even observed, through a telescope, smoke coming out of a filao-log cabin in the Colline district, others have noticed a smell of chicken curry. And there's even talk of roasted-joint leftovers and broken bottles being found in La Forêt du Brûlé.

Bourgeois militias are formed, ropes knotted, machetes honed. And yet it's less than three days since Marchand registered his complaint.

So what? All that's missing is the guilty man. Benches are hastily built for the trial, which will be packed. To the sound of nails being hammered, two camps form separate lines, running from Marchand's house to the court; on one side, the colonial aristocracy who swear that Edmond is guilty, on the other, the *engagés*, who maintain the opposite. Between the two lines comes Edmond, crossing the town with quaking steps, escorted by two gendarmes and Marchand, who, for the occasion, has donned his military uniform. No one knows where Edmond has come from, no one cares what he thinks.

We've got him! Let's throw him in prison.

And there Edmond remains for a week, from September 1 to 7, 1851.

On September 8, 1851, Edmond is taken, under escort, from the prison to the courthouse, where Joseph-Alphonse Moussoir, the examining magistrate, is preparing the cross-examination for the hearing while awaiting his arrival. A curious crowd is gathered in the courtroom. It's a case of theft after breaking and entering, with all possible and conceivable aggravating circumstances. To his defense lawyer, Edmond says almost nothing. To Moussoir, who asks a hundred questions, Edmond gives but one answer:

"Yes!"

Outrage on one side, shame on the other.

Yes, he stole a key, opened that box, stole the objects inside. Yes, he pleads guilty. Let's be done with him!

"The gallows!" impatient members of the public exhort.

"Clemency!" others attending entreat.

The judge turns to Edmond and asks him why he stole.

Crestfallen, head down, he doesn't answer. He's like a dog ashamed of his guilt, staring wide-eyed, looking embarrassed.

"Why did you steal?" the judge persists.

Edmond would like to hide under a pile of dead leaves with the ladybugs. The courtroom is huge, time has stopped. *Maman*, get me out of here! He can't recall having said *maman* before this day.

"Why? Speak up!"

"I . . . I . . . "

A mumble that only the universe can hear.

The judge gets annoyed.

"If all men plundered, stole what doesn't belong to them, where would the world be?"

Precisely where he is today, Edmond replies. In his head. Just to himself. Moussoir won't be any the wiser.

Later, the magistrate, Lepervanche, will write that Edmond had stolen due to the modesty of his wages, to buy himself a little of the comfort he'd had a taste of in the house of his former master. But from Edmond's mouth, no explanation will emerge. Perhaps he reckons that there'd be no point giving one. That the case was lost before it even began. The archives are empty, the minutes of his trial almost silent.

Edmond is but a shadow passing through the courthouse.

26
EDMOND GETS A PRISON SENTENCE
Jailhouse on Rue du Conseil, Saint-Denis, 1851-1852

*All the convicts double up laughing when Edmond says he's the
one who discovered how to hand-pollinate vanilla flowers.*

September 8, 1851, Edmond learns the term "committal
order" and returns to break rocks in the Saint-Denis jailhouse. He's not long turned twenty and he's just been
sentenced to five years of prison and chain work for the theft
of jewelry, seashells, and a roasted joint. He tells himself he's
pretty fortunate. Three years earlier, he'd have copped a volley
of cannon fire.

When the verdict was announced, he didn't react. When the
judge told him, in court, that he wouldn't get out before 1856, he
didn't cry. He didn't cry, either, in front of the iron door that the
prison guard opened wide to him. He'd been thinking of finish-
ing himself off with rum or cheap red in a hovel in the Bas de la
Rivière in any case. The warder didn't manhandle him. They've
been courteous enough to leave him alive since he's already dead.

From now on, Edmond lives surrounded by a crowd of de-
tainees, debtors, vagrants, lunatics who play the fiddle and dance
when they're not chasing after the chickens the janitor keeps in
the exercise yard. Vanilla? He's no longer even sure he'd know
how to pollinate it. Ferréol? There's been no further news for a
good two-and-a-half years. Perhaps their story is over.

To repay his debt to society, in both summer and winter,
Edmond digs paths, maintains roads, cleans out the Barachois
dock.[29] Otherwise, he works on building sites, helps with

[29] A basic harbor intended for just a few small boats.

land-clearance or gardening jobs. He thinks of nothing. He doesn't feel sorry for himself. At night, he only dreams a little, of being buried alive. By day, his life can be summed up as rock-breaking and foot-chains, a shirt, blue trousers, and seven hundred grams of rice, a bit less of dried vegetables or mashed cassava, locked inside a wooden lunch box.

His name is Edmond, the rest doesn't matter.

He no longer even knows what year or month it is. July maybe, because he's a bit cold. Unless it's already March. Since Edmond found and lost freedom, the calendar is of little importance.

Before, he would run in the gardens, eat *badamie* almonds, cracking them with his teeth, dive into the rivers. From now on, he's nothing but a convict among so many others, all Black or mulatto. You'd think crime has a color.

In his underworld beyond time, he did make a few friends. Trouabal, whose shirt no longer even hides the wide ulcer circling his chest; Renan, who talks to himself and cries at night when dreaming. Marthe, a former *Négresse d'habitation*, or domestic slave, who has a permanent limp because, for a year, she had to drag a weight of some twenty-five kilos around. "What did you do to get such a punishment?" he asks her when they first meet.

"*Missié Edmond, moin la casse trois z'assièt porcelaine de Sèvres.*"[30]

When the light has gone, and they are advancing slowly, groping in the air but unable to see their fingertips, they gather in a *rond'kozé*[31] made of old bits of canvas set around an extinguished firebox. There they pass the time exchanging amazing tales of an ocean that stretches between two worlds, with explorers and sea monsters with spiny fins; of vast prairies where

---

[30] "Monsieur Edmond, I broke three Sèvres porcelain plates."

[31] A place for debate.

ibis as big as ostriches run. But the convicts always double up laughing when Edmond says he's the one who discovered how to hand-pollinate vanilla flowers. There's just one man who doesn't laugh. That's old Ghislain, sorcerer and forger, a bit of a mythomaniac with visionary tendencies, who claims he can read the future in shooting stars and the seared wing of a bat.

One evening, when they are all in the prison yard gazing up at the star-studded sky, Ghislain speaks to Edmond. I see a locomotive moving around in underground tunnels like an earthworm. White walls. I see your name written in white on a blue rectangle. Thousands of people in black frock coats, a smell of urine, a population of horseback-riders. People riding horses without legs or rumps. A small board mounted on wheels, a swan's long neck, a metal beast moved forward with the aid of the foot. A school with your name, books, too . . .

And Edmond, who has had enough of this load of nonsense, slaps the soothsayer, who, clairvoyant though he is, didn't see it coming. The talking stops, the anger abates. Edmond, head resting on a stone closes his eyes as though on his deathbed. In spite of himself, he does look back on his cock-and-bull life. He's alone, and it's the solitude of a universe swarming with galaxies but empty of meaning. At twenty-three, he's already older than his father and nothing more than the child of his mother, a child who decided nothing, wanted nothing, to whom only life was given; life that clings like a sugar-gorged tick to the taste of blood.

Every three to four months, a convict escapes from the sieve-like prison and heads straight for the Bas de la Rivière. Edmond, who knows the way there, doesn't follow him, doesn't snitch on him. He wouldn't know what to do with freedom anymore. Every week, he's offered a glass of smuggled-in rum or wine. Edmond doesn't want alcohol. At most, he requests the most absurd, most witless thing the prisoners have ever heard of. He asks them to bring him a flower. And if there's any chance, if they can find one, a vanilla pod.

December 25, 1851. Edmond feels incredibly limp under a heap of ambitions. At nine in the evening, he becomes taut with bitterness and frustration. February 1852. Eleven at night, Edmond curses the days, hates this month. April 1852. Eleven-thirty at night, Edmond wonders whether you can become somebody when you're born nobody. So little joie de vivre, so many years to languish.

June 1852. Edmond can easily see himself dying in his prison as a lonely old man.

He falls asleep always dreaming the same dream. He's on a tomb. A stem of vanilla dances around the tombstone, forming a crown above the black hair of an unknown mother. From the east, a breeze blows that teases the leaves, a September blue wind that neither disturbs the waves nor diverts the clouds. Perhaps in a few months' time, at the height of the blazing-hot summer, this wind will turn into a cyclone. And then squalls from the ocean will sweep away the thatched roof, bend over the stalks of cane, strip the trees of their leaves, leaving a carpet of branches, ripe mangoes, and downy buds on the sodden ground. Some trees will huddle together, others suddenly fall after a century of resistance. Men, stooping and squinting, will struggle to advance through the gusts of wind. For now, it's but a light sea breeze, as harmless as a lily in a valley. And Edmond always hears, from the depths of his dream, this old message, dating back to the Bellevue vanilla nurseries:

Your flaws won't engulf you,
fears won't dig you grave!
But still, you'll have to wait.[32]

---

[32] Final line spoken in a hushed voice in Edmond's dream.

27
EDMOND GETS OUT OF JAIL
The north of the island of Bourbon, 1852-1855

Edmond, come outside!

Four leagues from the prison, through a half-open window, the night breeze slides like a snake into Ferréol's bedroom. It slithers along the walls, up the four wooden bedposts, swells the drapes behind which he's gently awakening. Ferréol has just been dreaming of Edmond. He calls it an obsession, Elvire calls it remorse. On the bed's drapes he sees Edmond running. At two months, two years, ten, eleven years old. The truth is, he has the same dream every night. There was once a slave who found some treasure that masters stole from him. The masters grew richer, the slave died. From January to December, Ferréol shouts himself hoarse, tosses and turns, wakes up the entire neighborhood with his weird dreams. That court that imprisoned Edmond, maybe it sentenced him, too.

It's a little chilly, and Ferréol, lying on his back, hands on belly, makes a big decision. He just cannot keep waking with a start anymore, face haggard, sheets on the floor, peace of mind gone. At past midnight, and over sixty-one years of age, Ferréol vows to mend what has been broken in Edmond.

For a couple of years, a ghastly fever of forgiveness and amnesty has been blighting Bourbon. The courts seem more like confessionals, the magistrates grant pardons left, right, and center. For the utterly guilty, the finest excuses are found. Ferréol hopes that Edmond will forgive everything, and for that he intends to get him out of jail. Still in his woolen nightcap, by the light of a feeble lamp, Ferréol writes a letter to Justin Béret, public prosecutor of La Réunion. He defends the young man who discovered how to hand-pollinate vanilla, requests an easing of his sentence and state remuneration for him. He explains that Edmond, more than anyone, deserves public recognition and the government's clemency.

A few days before Shrove Tuesday, Ferréol's letter makes its way through the corridors of the courthouse and lands on Justin Béret's desk.

"And why not the Légion d'honneur, too?" the public prosecutor splutters. "Merely for the fruit of the vanilla plant, he should be pardoned?"

Justin Béret, who loves only dishes with sauces and fine wines, has never liked vanilla or chocolate. On April 6, 1852, without rereading the letter, he files it away in an old cardboard box and sends a rejection note to Monsieur Beaumont.

In Sainte-Suzanne, Ferréol screws up the reply and issues a call to arms. He raises a small battalion of accomplices armed with writing paper and inkpots. For hours and months, they write, erase, screw up, restart letters they mean to bombard the public prosecutor and Governor with. There are now four of them signing letters that Béret barely reads. As well as Ferréol, there's Lepervanche, Volcy-Focard, and Elvire. They defend the idea that Edmond Albius is among those former slaves whom an ill-prepared freedom truly drove to crime. They swear that his defense at court was flawed, that his value outweighs his offence. They write of attenuating circumstances, penal irresponsibility, and a host of other things that the prosecutor doesn't take in. Unfortunately for him, not a week goes by now without a letter to him from Ferréol requesting that Edmond's sentence be revised.

November 1852, Justin Béret takes stock. On his desk, he gathers up sixty-three letters asking for Edmond's release, five anonymous letters threatening to reveal to the world, and to his wife Germaine, his supposed liaison with a Creole from

Montgaillard if he doesn't pardon Edmond at once. He also has twenty-four requests for an immediate meeting from a collective of vanilla growers on the east of the island.

December 1852, public prosecutor Béret plunges yet again into this morass of requests. He frowns, reads each letter, one by one. Finally, he finds the only missive he was looking for: an invitation card to the jamboree organized by the Governor.

Since August 8, 1852, Bourbon has boasted a very special representative of the State: Louis Henri Hubert Delisle, the first Governor who is native to the island, a child of Saint-Benoît. Hubert Delisle arrived on the frigate *La Belle-Poule* with his wife Amélina. As he disembarks at around half past three, Hubert Delisle is moved to see thousands of Bourbon islanders who have come to the pebble beach of Barachois to welcome him. They chant his name, recite poems by his friend Lamartine, cover the blue of the sea with yellow allamanda petals, from flowers specially picked for his arrival. In a rash outburst, Hubert Delisle cries: "*Mi aime zot toute!*" I love you all. He promises that he'll support the *engagés*, and all the oppressed of the Earth, and then hastens to his office to regret what he's just said.

On December 8, 1853, Hubert Delisle nearly chokes as he reads three letters reminding him of his promise on arrival. The first is from Ferréol Beaumont, who is asking for a pardon to be granted to his former slave Edmond Albius, and thus, for himself, the right to sleep in peace. To help the Governor decide, he attaches two kilos of vanilla to his request. The second letter is the one from Béret, imploring him to free this Edmond because he has no room left on his desk or in his cupboard to store all the letters and boxes of vanilla he receives regarding the matter. The last and longest missive is from Lepervanche, magistrate of Sainte-Suzanne. In a letter accompanied by five vanilla pods, he portrays Edmond as a black Jussieu, an African Linnaeus, a native of the east of the island like him, to whom we owe the discovery of how to hand-pollinate vanilla flowers, a new branch of horticulture that has revolutionized the vanilla trade worldwide, no less!

Monsieur le Gouverneur,

I am taking the liberty of making a request to you on behalf of a poor Black condemned to five years in the galleys.

But this unfortunate man has every right to this recommendation and to the gratitude of the country. The discovery of how to pollinate vanilla flowers is down to him alone, and thus it is to him alone that the colony is indebted for this new branch of horticulture, destined to be greatly expanded, and already widespread in the Vent region.

At the time of the institution of the Fête du Travail [. . .], I was soliciting from the Commissaire Général, Sarda Garriga, state remuneration for this young Black.

To this effect, I presented a request to him, which was passed on to the Directeur de l'intérior, in whose office it has remained forgotten.

The inventor of the process for pollinating the vanilla flower was of even more interest at that time than today, since he hadn't yet lost the esteem of decent people, and it is even possible that if, from then, the Government had accorded him the remuneration that would have shielded him from need, he wouldn't have turned to crime to satisfy the tastes he acquired at the home of his former master, who had treated him more like his son than his slave, and of whom he was, in common parlance, the spoilt child.

Edmond lost his mother at birth.

Etc.

Etc.

Please take all of these grounds into consideration,

Monsieur le Gouverneur, and promise me that you will kindly seek the pardon of this interesting and unfortunate young man from His Majesty the Emperor of the French.

Confident in your recognized qualities of humanity and generosity, I dare to hope that you will grant my request.

I am honored to be, Monsieur le Gouverneur, your humble and obedient servant.

The Magistrate,
Lepervanche Mézières,
Sainte-Suzanne, December 8, 1853.[33]

Hubert Delisle means to deal with this matter without delay, pops the three letters into his "urgent complaints" tray, and goes off to open Bourbon's first colonial industry fair: a marquee with a turbine on display and miniature sugar refineries, the crowning of the best cane-cutter, and a competition to find the finest Moka bullock. While he's away, the wind half-opens the door leading to the garden, teases the flowers on his desk, shuffles some papers, then withdraws, while an official passing in the corridor asks firmly, "Who goes there?" The wind settles, all innocent. The official is just moving off when a sudden gust opens the shutters with a clatter. A squall shakes the table and lifts the letters. They fly off through the window, swirl above the trees, sweep over the street, and end their mad rush in the sea. Upon his return, Hubert Delisle, noticing that the letters have gone, presumes that his secretary has dealt with the file, and so focuses on all his other business. He tours the villages and towns, fancies himself the Baron Haussmann of the tropics, designs bridges and tunnels,

---

[33] A transcription in the *Archives de Bourbon no. 10*, a letter from Mézières Lepervanche to the Governor, December 8, 1853.

talks of a public library, inaugurates the main road encircling the island, right along the coast.

Everyone applauds this tireless Governor, who sleeps little, works too much, and prides himself on knowing all the eminent families of the island. The months go by, buildings go up, roads are dug, but it's no good! Hubert Delisle has the feeling of having done something badly. Until, that is, the day when, in front of a dish of vanilla ice cream, he remembers the *engagé* Edmond Albius, asks after him, chokes on hearing the answer. By then it is 1855, sixteen months, two weeks, and a few days since Lepervanche sent his letter to the Governor. And it has been three years, seven months, and twenty-seven days that Edmond has been in prison. Hubert Delisle demands that he be pardoned at once.

On April 26, 1855, at around five thirty in the morning, as darkness is fading, a star lights up in Edmond's heart. For him, finally, the ordeal of what is politely called the slowness of French administration is coming to an end. Thanks to a dish of vanilla ice cream, he is released from jail. Released for good behavior on the Governor's orders. Once again, he notes that he owes something to vanilla. Edmond isn't looking lovely as a lily; he doesn't smell of roses, rather of salted cod and boiled cabbage. His face has aged prematurely. He's like an angel with broken wings. He breathes in the aroma of the Rue du Conseil, that blend of dew and frangipani trees mingled with the first rays of sunshine. Edmond is glad. Lost, too. Because he has nowhere to go. He sits right down in the dust and, for the first time in his life, he cries.

A few meters away from him, there's a handcart, left there by a fruit-and-vegetable merchant the previous day, and a cart attached to two oxen. With his face wet from convulsive sobbing, Edmond doesn't see that, close to the merchant's huge tarp, something is stirring. At first, he thinks he's hearing the rumbling of his stomach. Ahem! Ahem! Ahem! Someone coughed close to the cart. Edmond sits up, his heart racing. Suddenly, emerging from under the tarp, is Volcy-Focard, now chief clerk at the appellate court; then comes Lepervanche, still a magistrate, still a good man; followed by Elvire, adoptive aunt; and finally, Aristide Patu de Rosemont, town-council man and landowner. All friends of his former master. He daren't say his own friends. With straw in their disheveled hair, they all surround Edmond, who's jumping around like a kid goat. He's just spent three years that felt like three centuries in a deathtrap, and all he can find to say is: "*Oté! Mi té attend pas! Où sa i lé Ferréol?*" He wasn't expecting them, no; and where is Ferréol?

Ferréol, after three years of insomnia, has fallen asleep under the tarp, between a sack of potatoes and seventeen kilos of zucchini. Ferréol is three centuries and seven years late, but he's most definitely there. Hearing the cries of joy, he sits up, claims he wasn't asleep, almost falls as he gets down from the cart, his cheeks still dusty from the potatoes. With a beard thick as fur, and countless wrinkles, his sight is going and he is hard of hearing. He's sixty-three and his joints are painful. He lands in Edmond's arms, which are thin as a fakir's, weeps enough to exhaust everyone and, getting his words mixed up, says "son" when others might have said "Edmond."

28
EDMOND BECOMES A GROWER
Sainte-Suzanne, 1855-1862

World! Here I am!

His name is Edmond, and he's one of a small group of the penniless who grabbed destiny by the horns before it gored them. His name is Edmond Albius, and he's certain that without vanilla, his life would be worse than it is, that vanilla is his lucky star, the undeniable presence of his mother and his ancestors. He's twenty-six, and appears twenty years older thanks to his many gray hairs, his thick moustache, his drooping shoulders, but is doggedly determined to forge ahead, despite the chilly Saint-Denis morning, the huge street, and this new feeling of freedom all intimidating him. He daren't say so to his friends, but they know everything and understand. So they take him by the hand and lead him to Sainte-Suzanne, where it all began.

On April 26, 1855, Edmond is back treading the soil of his native town when a group of schoolboys, directed by Brothers Scubilion and Vétérin, take to the stage erected in front of a small house. Before an audience of eight, in a playlet, they act out Edmond's life, his birth in a barn, his role as gardener's assistant, the discovery of vanilla, the ordeal of his trial. Three massive pasteboard facades represent the main locations and events in his life. There's the barn, its entrance looking out towards Ferréol's and Elvire's homes, the vanilla nursery, the prison on the Rue du Conseil. There's also a baby's rattle, his certificate of emancipation, and a full-length pencil portrait of Linnaeus. There are even a few small branches from around the Délices waterfall where, at seven, Edmond caught his first grouper fish.

Most of all, there's vanilla, four to five meters of creepers that are still green.

On the stage, to Edmond's right, a lectern supports about a hundred pages, symbolizing all the manuals, treatises, belongings of Ferréol that Edmond carried around, and the former's never-completed Plants of Bourbon encyclopedia. To his left, there's a human cavalry of hostile slaves, armed with wooden sabers and convicts' curses, envious of Edmond's discovery and ready to do battle with him. Suddenly, after an invisible, and entirely symbolic, raising of the curtain, a little Cafre, bold as a peacock, bursts out of a big hessian sack, presumably Mélise's body, shouting: "World! Here I am!" He cries out, rolls around on the floor, hoes an invisible kitchen garden, picks a giant, very real pumpkin, and fiddles with some lady's-slipper orchids. The scene in which Edmond discovers how to hand-pollinate vanilla is improbably tense. The spectators sit up, mouths agape, hands clasped, and, like him, all lean in the same direction, like a tree bowed by the wind. The grand finale of the show is the small cry, a kind of raucous and warlike "Owww!" that the botanist Edmond—played by a little Congolese freed slave—lets out as he falls to his knees, his right hand on his heart, a vanilla pod in his left hand, while declaring it was all "For France!" Ferréol has tears in his eyes. At the end of the play, all the guests stand up, open-mouthed, hands burning from applauding so much. Two schoolboys do such a good impression of the cannon shots of December 20 that Elvire thinks for a moment that the English have landed once again.

There's weeping, more applauding, stamping of feet, and Edmond, moved himself, asks for a handkerchief so no one sees his moist eyes. The show is drawing to a close.

A child then arrives with a rolled-up painting tied with velvet ribbon.

"C'est pour ou, missié Edmond." It is for him, for Edmond.

Edmond opens it out to find a portrait of himself so ugly that he recoils: the head is twice as small as it should be, the nostrils four times bigger than required, the eyebrows bushy, the jacket buttons ready to burst, the feet too wide, the hands hideous. But by now, carried away by the spirited performances, he's lost all objectivity and declares this horror the loveliest gift he's ever been given since the rattle and cow's bladder Elvire gave him. The portrait is passed from hand to hand, striking such terror in everyone that they dream of it that night.

Finally, urged on by Ferréol, Edmond stands up and stammers a few words: Ferréol is his *ti père*, these performers exceptional, Scubilion worthy of beatification. All the actors then gather on the stage.

Edmond hugs each pupil, calls them "my little ones." Elvire then brings over a ginormous pound cake with orange icing, to go with faham-orchid and vanilla tea. Performers and spectators polish it all off in a few seconds, without drawing breath. The children then head back to Saint-Benoît in a cart driven by Scubilion. Edmond runs alongside it for a few meters, waving and crying out, "My children, thank you, my children!"

When Edmond turns back, he sees a little house five meters from a mango tree, set on a plot of land planted with egret orchids, corn, and sweet potatoes. It is now his. His friends are lending it to him—they say giving, but Edmond, very embarrassed, insists that it be just a loan. Deep inside, he thinks that this house is the consecration of his life, his true accomplishment. Finally some land that's really his, on which he'll be both planter and botanist!

From the window of this house of a single large room, he can see Ferréol's house, and the familiar vista so reassures him that he seeks nothing beyond it. He purses his lips and rubs his eyelids, blaming the dust. Since it stings everyone's eyes, as if they were all in a sand storm coming from the Sahara, ten thousand leagues away, they all pull out handkerchiefs to wipe their eyes and blow their noses, because real men, it's well known, mustn't cry.

Having been a stone-cutter, and at least ten other unmentionable things, Edmond becomes a grower and day laborer. He goes back and forth between his home and Ferréol's, whom he helps in countless ways; his home and Elvire's, who showers him with clothes, cakes, affection, so much so that one day, meaning to call her *ti tante*, his tongue slips and he says *ti mère*.

All week long, Edmond, with trousers rolled up to his knees, lugs bundles of kindling for the fire in his kitchen. Next, he transforms his land from stony ground into a kitchen garden. He plants a coffee tree here, some banana palms there. All the crops that merchants pay a small fortune for—cloves, capsicums, cotton, and indigo—flourish on Edmond's land. Three times a year, he helps Ferréol's sow deliver a litter of ten piglets, each weighing in at one kilo thirty, never more, never less. Edmond will give some to Volcy-Focard, Lepervanche, and close neighbors. And he won't forget Isidore, now a carpenter, who visits him every week.

After all that, Edmond will devote himself to what he loves most: the orchids.

29
ANTOINE LOUIS ROUSSIN, LITHOGRAPHER
Artist's studio, 1862-1863

And that's how Edmond's appearance became known, at a time when men didn't yet know how to laugh heartily because they didn't suspect that happiness might exist.

At around the same time, an infantry sergeant disembarked from a three-master with one hundred and seventy-four canons, loaded with naval officers, sea biscuits, and convicts. He was carrying a cumbersome object that, shortly after, gossips described as special, magical, and potentially dangerous. It was, in fact, merely his military file, which described him thus:

> *Antoine Roussin, born March 3, 1819, in Avignon, sergeant in the 3rd marine infantry regiment. Average size, brown eyes, aquiline nose, broad forehead. Suspect element: passion for painting, drawing and lithography.*

Once he had fulfilled his military contract, Antoine Roussin moved into a light-filled house with a glass roof, close to the church in Saint-Benoît. He called the back room his studio, and set about turning himself into a photographer-lithographer.

At first, he had not a friend, visitor, or client. He could be heard leaving the studio at dawn and returning several days later, along with a panting assistant lugging a large wooden trunk. After a few weeks, he stopped leaving his studio; the neighbors might have thought he'd died or emigrated had he not been heard banging all day long on a wooden partition, with three nails between his teeth and a carpenter's hammer in his fist. At first, due to excessive noise, the vicinity of his house was avoided. Then a former convict turned policeman was sent to investigate the racket. He entered and stopped in the doorway. Behind him, a first man, following him closely, slowed down. Then a second man. Soon, the entire neighborhood was gathered outside Roussin's studio, so that even the teak parquet was no longer visible. Before a crowd all wondering what a photographer-lithographer actually was, Roussin calmly prepared some silver-covered copper plates, two varnished-wood boxes, cotton, and albumen paper, then solemnly declared that this apparatus, having received the praise of Louis-Napoléon, was reserved for the island's seriously rich. Next, he stretched a long white sheet between two bamboo supports, ushered the curious to stand in front of it, walked back thirty paces, and leaned over the apparatus. In front of him, no one moved anymore, the children held tight by their mothers, the men stock-still and open-mouthed. All were waiting for something or other to come out of this Pandora's box, maybe a rapid and deadly burst of artillery fire. Facing them, Antoine Roussin, who still had them in his sights, remained silent and equally still. After thirty minutes that seemed an eternity to them, he finally straightened up, his eye ringed with black, and pushed everyone out of his studio.

The following week, the newspaper announced an exhibition of photographs and lithographs at Roussin's studio. Once again, the crowd squeezed in. The studio walls were hung with photographs of the church, the Grand Étang, the flowing waters of the La Paix basin. And then there was a photograph of the neighbors gathered around the policeman. Resounding applause erupted. People marveled out loud at this painting done in barely thirty minutes without a paintbrush.

From then on, there was a thriving business in portraits in the east of the island. On Roussin's studio wall there were pictures of bourgeois families who had come from all the towns and villages of the Côte-au-Vent to be photographed. Soon, all of Bourbon was clamoring for Roussin to tour the island.

One morning, in his painting studio, Roussin is moaning to his wife, Marie Louise Élisabeth Petit, a Creole woman who has given him five children, all of whom hate his portraits. I can do better! he declares. And so he leaves Saint-Benoît for Saint-Denis. A few weeks later, he loads wife, children, pencils, and sketchbooks into a small cart and travels around the island, from coast to coast. He's working on a large album on La Réunion, a self-indulgent medley that he imagines in four volumes, combining the flora and fauna, landscapes, neighborhoods, different ethnic groups, and the most emblematic men and occupations of the island. Roussin pesters the puppeteers, bread-roll sellers, *jacquots malbars* street performers, clothes-menders, and local urchins, the *marmailles désordeurs*. On the smallest village square, the slightest church parvis, beside the lowliest fountain, he could be seen standing quite still, photographing or drawing. Nearby, there would be Marie Louise Élisabeth Petit chasing after four children, one up a tree, another at the back of a cart, two others tugging on the skirts of a camellia seller, and all with the fifth asleep in her arms. Soon the album is published in instalments and the Roussin-Petit couple is in pieces. You can't have it all.

One morning, Ferréol sees an advertisement in the newspaper:

Those wishing to have their portraits lithographed should contact Monsieur Roussin, who guarantees a resemblance and is offering twenty-five copies for the sum of a hundred francs. In Saint-Denis, contact Monsieur A. Roussin, rue du Barachois.

It's a chance to make Edmond known, because many may have heard of him thanks to vanilla, but few have seen him. Talking of vanilla, the island has just set a record by exporting four tons of it. The taste for vanilla is even spreading across the French colonies in Africa and Asia. Ferréol considers

Edmond to be one of the outstanding figures of 19th-century La Réunion. Roussin is delighted to do his portrait. And that's how Edmond's appearance became known, at a time when men didn't yet know how to laugh heartily before the shutter of a camera or the gaze of an artist with a pencil, because they didn't suspect that happiness might exist.

What remains is a lithograph of Edmond, made in 1862 and accompanied by a notice written by the clerk of the court Volcy-Focard. A portrait with a caption is a small but important innovation at that time. The following year, the *Album de l'île de La Réunion*, published by Antoine Louis Roussin, includes this portrait of Edmond Albius.

He is wearing a light-colored shirt under a gray or white heavy-cotton jacket, as though, on this tropical island, there was always a touch of winter within him. A scarf knotted like a bowtie around his neck gives him an elegant and dignified air. His trousers are dark as the ocean separating Bourbon from the possible Mozambique of his ancestors. He has a smooth, long face, somewhat angular, somewhat rectangular, hollow cheeks divided by a flat nose above a bushy moustache and tiny beard. His thick eyebrows and narrow forehead give him rather deep-set eyes, of which the snowy whites contrast with the dark irises. His blank expression reveals little of a life of toil, of destitution. His left hand holds a vanilla flower so white it's luminous. Behind him there are vanilla pods, light-colored fleshy leaves on creepers climbing tightly around a tree trunk—a coconut palm—and, in the distance, a rural landscape of fields dotted with copses. Edmond is thirty-three, appears older. Behind the mask of the mute adult, seeming old and tired, there's a glimpse of the wily and mischievous child he once was. He stares straight at the artist, looking serious, devoid of curiosity, his frizzy black hair abundant and neatly styled. He doesn't look happy, he doesn't seem unhappy, he is not of the race of men who complain. In the image as in life, he is alone but redeemed.

30
CLAUDE RICHARD
Jardin du Roy, 1862

La vanille, c'est lui![34]

La vanille, c'est moi!"—I *am* vanilla!

It is with these words that Jean Michel Claude Richard screws up the *Moniteur de l'île Bourbon*, after reading that Antoine Roussin has just done a portrait of the former slave Edmond Albius that will soon appear in his *Album de l'île de La Réunion*.

Claude Richard arrives on Bourbon in the early 1830s. He has never known either destitution or glory, living, like the majority of men, somewhere in between, without exceptional happiness or excessive regret. Some gardens bear his name; he is now in charge of the Jardin du Roy, a vast tree-filled park located at the heart of Saint-Denis, Bourbon's main town. Claude Richard, who wants for nothing, has a big problem all the same. He is one of those men who not only demands to be in the limelight, but also refuses for it to shine on anyone else. A curt man with an inscrutable face, he has never been known to smile. His family? A wife, Caroline, to whom he has virtually stopped speaking. Richard is aging badly. The plants in his kitchen garden are dying, along with his prestige. He fears going down in history for the wrong reasons.

When it comes to Blacks, he's encountered hundreds—water-carriers, agricultural workers, good-for-nothings, drudgers. He came across Edmond with Ferréol, when he was a slave of around ten at most and would help him, on various occasions,

---

[34] He *is* vanilla!

by carrying bags of seeds, or cuttings. Claude Richard is fifty-five when Edmond discovers how to hand-pollinate vanilla. He can't believe that it's a child, even worse, a slave, who has unlocked vanilla's secret.

"A Black! A Black!" he screams at his wife. "Impossible! Unthinkable!"

By what process, and over how many years, Claude Richard moves from "it's impossible" to "it's me who taught him how to do it," no one knows. Ferréol knows only that what Richard couldn't prevent he decided to attribute to himself.

Early one Monday morning, Richard organizes Bourbon's first press conference, serving coffee beside the carp pond in the Jardin du Roy. In front of an audience of journalists, who leave no sugar at the bottom of their cups, he claims that the time has come to reveal the truth. It is he who taught everything to Edmond!

The so-called news immediately travels right around Bourbon, in a clockwise direction. In the east, it is rigidly maintained that Edmond is the veritable discoverer. In the west, the opposite is maintained. Between the two, Edmond slowly shakes his head from right to left, touching his smooth forehead with his right hand. He doesn't lose his temper anymore, doesn't frown anymore. He no longer lets an ordeal get to him. In this land of constraint and mud, he now knows that the slightest success of a slave is a contravention that leads to disputes and usurpations. Even twenty years later.

Edmond is no longer on the warpath; from now on, he doesn't give a damn about vainglory.

And anyhow, he has Ferréol's full support. Throughout December 1862, Ferréol sends letters to the chief clerk of the court, Eugène Volcy-Focard, asking him to help him to defend Edmond's honor. He also writes to Claude Richard, telling him that there's one thing he must understand: he, Edmond, *is* vanilla. He alone. And that's all there is to it.

On December 9, 1862, Ferréol is over seventy when he sends a final request regarding Edmond to the Governor. He encloses with it Roussin's lithograph captioned by Volcy-Focard. He hopes that that will finally persuade him to grant state remuneration to his dear Albius.

We lose trace of Ferréol in September 1863. He is seventy-one and, as recorded in the *Archives de Bourbon,* sends an umpteenth letter to Volcy-Focard. "Edmond has asked me to convey his thanks to Monsieur Roussin for the lithographs he kindly sent, along with the one that was for me. The ingenious inventor of the pollination of vanilla was, indeed, able to pass some on to his relatives and friends, great lovers of drawings and engravings, like all the Blacks." Ferréol concludes by describing his ailments and how Edmond has become his factotum.

Of the hundreds of letters Ferréol writes and sends, this is the last one Edmond knows about. This is where the shared story of Edmond and Ferréol ends, childless botanists both who, thanks to vanilla, created life, having never been able to give life otherwise.

Ferréol dies, we imagine, of old age in a bed watched over by Elvire. A thirty-four-year-old Edmond holds his hand. Undoubtedly, Ferréol's close relatives and his oldest friends, Volcy-Focard and Lepervanche, are there. It's possible that Isidore attends the funeral, albeit reluctantly. Ferréol's godchildren may not come since they live in Paris, Dijon, Tonnerre, and don't fancy boarding a frigate loaded with salted pork and live sheep for three months of seasickness and the corpse of a botanist uncle. Whatever the case, on that particular day, Edmond placed one knee on the ground and wept like never before.

Once more an orphan and without a home, Edmond now feels the supportive hand of the director of clerks' offices, Eugène Volcy-Focard, on his shoulder. He has just lost a father, he finds an adoptive uncle. Until his death, Volcy-Focard never stops speaking about Edmond's fate to the vanilla growers of Bourbon and asking that justice be done. "Would not our vanilla-nursery owners accomplish an act of reparation if they each deducted a few vanilla pods from the next harvest for the benefit of Edmond Albius? It wouldn't require a great quantity to secure for him, in the Hauts de Sainte-Suzanne where he lives, a straw roof and a few *gaulettes* of land to cultivate?"[35]

It would seem that certain vanilla growers think yes, but most of them say no.

[35] Volcy-Focard, "Introduction et fécondation de la vanille à Bourbon," *Dix-huit mois de République à l'Île Bourbon*, Saint-Denis, Lahuppe, 1863, pp. 248-257.

31
THE MEETING OF EDMOND AND MARIE-PAULINE BASSANA
Commune-Carron, 1869

Something warms up inside him, something that was dry and cold, desert and darkness. Edmond, wounded in a war called life, begins to smile again beside a woman.

All that Edmond knows of family, of botany, of father-son relations comes to him from Ferréol. When he dies, Edmond realizes that he knows nothing of the love between a man and a woman. All his life he has been surrounded by bachelors, spinsters, and dead loves. At sixteen, he still thought that babies came out of the belly button. There had been that day when, like everyone, he had hugged the trunk of a tree and, on an impulse he'd been ashamed of, had kissed it three times in a row, like he'd seen Grand-Marron do to Colombine. Edmond had closed his eyes and puckered up, more to know how it felt than out of conviction. But the coconut palms weren't his type. At around twenty, he had certainly attended a few *bals la poussière*, whispered sweet nothings in a field of spuds, but he had never known anything other than fleeting secret loves. Of the two women he could have loved, one had died of tuberculosis, the other had married Isidore.

Otherwise, love had never rung out in his life like the church bells do on Sunday. He had even imagined love to be something pretty dangerous, almost cursed, since his parents had died of it, as had Ferréol's wife. In his eyes, it was just silly women's fodder, served with tantrums, sulks lasting several weeks, and huge misunderstandings that were still hard to digest twenty years later. Worse, it left men lonely and miserable.

The bachelor Edmond makes do with his fingers and hands,

which, so all the pumpkin and vanilla flowers say, work wonders. In any case, he believes he has neither the face to be desired, nor the heart to love.

And yet, at the dawn of his fortieth year, Edmond is on the verge of changing his mind. For some time, his heart has been hurting him. A strange sound keeps coming out of it. One evening, Edmond decides to make a long cylinder by tying a roll of paper, then, stretching out like a starfish with his back in the dust, he sticks one end of it against his chest, with the other end touching his ear. In Le Havre, a certain Dr. Laennec, passionate about pulmonary diseases and the flute, had treated his father with a similarly strange object made of a cylinder of hollow wood. He had given it an equally strange name. Horoscope, telescope, stethoscope, Edmond can't quite remember. Ferréol told him this story such a long time ago. He can hear his own breathing, the beating of his heart. Lying under a large tamarind tree, its yellow, red-veined flowers falling like snowflakes around his ears, he listens over and over again to the sounds from his chest, muted, light, short. Clearly, something's not right. From then on, every evening, Edmond listens to his sluggish heart and frets. Elvire, watching this strange routine from her window, calls out to him and questions him. After a month of this rigmarole, Edmond comes up with his own diagnosis: he isn't sick, there's not the slightest hint of a heart murmur. He could make all the cylinders in the world, they would just endlessly send back to him the echo of his own loneliness.

Just like a doctor, Edmond makes up a prescription for himself, a treatment for life: a wife with a low voice whose ylang-ylang or jasmine perfume would smother the smell of meat juices, gamey *tangue*, and pea puree that wafts out of his kitchen. Tall or short, fat or ugly, he couldn't care less. It will be enough that this woman loves him. That very evening, as though coming from the depths of the universe, two comets trace a path towards the east of the island, and shoot over his head. Silently, Edmond makes a wish. To fall in love.

While waiting for love—that which you must never look for, that just falls on you like a coconut off a branch—Edmond cultivates the land by day, and reads *Graziella* by night. This novel by Lamartine had been given to him by the Governor, Hubert Delisle, in recognition of his contribution to the global economy. Ferréol had already read the whole book to him two or three times. Then Edmond had learnt to read it on his own, or rather, had memorized it off by heart. In front of any other text, he was totally illiterate. But with *Graziella*, he drank in every word, in little sips, alone. While reading it, he had experienced what felt like a great punch in the face. Since then, he had taken up fishing, coral carving, and believed in the existence of Italy, the muscat grape, and Venice. Edmond became what is called a faithful reader because, for a full eight years, he read the same book. Eight pages every day. A rereading every month. And every final evening of the month, for eight years, he would close his only novel, the eternal *Graziella*, exclaiming: roll on next month! Ninety-six readings, accompanied by as many prayers, to find his own Graziella. In Sainte-Suzanne, if possible. Because Naples was, frankly, not within his means. The years passed, then the decades. Much as Edmond searched, all he ended up with was a reputation for being a rather odd, that's to say, obsessive, loner, because fiddling only with vanilla, reading only one novel, waiting for only one woman doesn't tend to make one appear normal, even in the 19th century.

1869. Edmond is a bachelor of forty centuries, or maybe forty years old. He looks like a hunchbacked sixty-year-old, his back as stooped as if the world's troubles were weighing down on it. He has read *Graziella* almost a hundred times, in floods of tears the last three times. His heart is worn out like a cobblestone. That's enough, he'll read no more! For this evening, at least. He remembers the demonstration happening at the Bassanas' place, gets up and heads off to pay them a visit in Commune-Carron.

When Edmond arrives at the courtyard, the entire neighborhood is there for what's almost a show. In a burst of opportunism, Paranton Bassana, a minor grower and great showman, is speaking with expansive gestures about a machine that's come from New York, via the Paris trade fair, and will revolutionize fashion, sewing, the lives of women, the appearance of men.

"Look! There it is! The island's very first one!"

On a table, entirely shrouded in a white-wool sheet, the thing looks like a little ghost quietly waiting to surprise its world. In the role of his assistant is Françoise Avallon, his wife, the mother of four children of whom two are corpses, because vaccines are still rare and smallpox common. Very gently, she removes the sheet and, to the dumbfounded crowd, presents a black machine embellished with white curlicues. Four kilos of metal that, with a worrying clickety-clack, transform any old rag into a princess's gown.

"So that's a sewing machine?"

Without waiting for the answer, everyone crowds around this object in the form of a large pistol, equipped with a needle below, a reel of thread above, and a handle at the back.

"They say it works on coal and steam. And it pricks the finger like a cactus!"

Other rumors then come thick and fast about the results of the machine, which everyone fiddles with, weighs up, and wants to see working. Marie-Pauline Bassana, the daughter of Paranton and Françoise, who is still without work but soon to become a seamstress, prepares to give a demonstration, while her father brings over some lace and her mother a reel of thread. Voice, figure, hair, Edmond recognizes them immediately, despite being eight years late. A heart starts to beat again in his old brain.

"Graziella, I bet!"

She had replied "Marie-Pauline," because betting was a practice less respectable than doing laundry or basket-weaving. Edmond had persisted.

"No, no, Graziella."

Marie-Pauline alias Graziella, officially without work, is eighteen; Edmond is twenty-two years older. To make up for this gap, he now won't be apart from her for a single day. On Monday, Edmond has a tear in his trousers; Tuesday, some hemming to be done; Wednesday, his sheet needs mending. The months fly by and, by day, Marie-Pauline patches up linen that Edmond then unpicks by night. Paranton, not smart enough to work out this mustachioed Penelope's ruse, but too shrewd not to see Edmond coming, opens up one evening to his wife, who tells him to let it lie.

Lie, die, Paranton, after nineteen years of marriage and a little less of deafness, isn't sure he quite heard the word said by his wife, and, alas, it's her last word. Françoise Avallon leaves everything, both the quest for happiness and doubts about death, to go off and live one of those new lives that her Indian husband swears, on the *Bhagavad Gita*, really do exist. It is July 6, 1869, and Françoise Avallon, after forty-one years of spade and soil, drops into it like a seed that everyone, including Edmond, waters with tears.

He will replace her in the heart of her daughter, and in the kitchen garden, too, because, say what you like, cabbages and carrots don't grow on their own.

No doubt Paranton would ignore Edmond if he wasn't the one who had discovered vanilla, as they say here. No doubt Marie-Pauline would reject him if he didn't woo her with bunches of hydrangeas and little boxes of vanilla smelling of honey and spices that he places beside the sewing machine. Marie-Pauline's little brother Simon, with all the wisdom of his sixteen years, thinks it's the portrait of Edmond by Antoine Roussin given to his sister that finally won her round. But no one's interested in the opinion of a spiteful, adolescent gravedigger.

There had been another decisive episode. On a Sunday picnic beside the river, when the sudden rise in the water had taken everyone by surprise. Paranton, still on the other bank, had wanted to cross but had fallen into the river with a resounding splash. He was starting to take in great gulps of water. Simon and Marie-Pauline were running in all directions, as were the currents. Anyone who can swim, jump in! No one could. Edmond, who wasn't a strong swimmer, had still dived into the river and swum, swum, and swum some more to reach Paranton, and then dragged him by his billowing shirt. The story had ended well. Since that day, there had been a kind of covenant, an undying bond sealed forever with an embrace. They had become father-in-law and son-in-law, had spat on the ground, with right hands raised. Nothing would part them ever again.

August 1870. Rumors of war between France and Prussia shake the island of La Réunion. Edmond wonders whether, at forty, he can still be of any use. He's a bachelor with nothing left to lose, not even any revenge to take. On the market square, a town crier reads a few lines from a new novel by Victor Hugo:

> I come to warn you. I come to denounce your happiness. It is made of the unhappiness of other people. You have everything, and this everything consists of the nothing of others.[36]

Edmond is amazed that this gentleman from France uses words that seem to be written for him. Is it a sign that he must join this nation at war?

France, that's where all the vanilla pods go that Bourbon

---

[36] Victor Hugo, *L'Homme qui rit*, A. Lacroix, Verboeckhoven & Cie, 1869.

has been exporting since he was thirteen. He imagines the place as a procession of frock coats, a republic of wide avenues that powdered men, cane in hand, stroll along. He might meet Alexandre Dumas, take Italian classes with Lamartine. Edmond wants to enlist.

He changes his mind when he learns that soldiers must pay their own passage, and that, a few houses away, Elvire has just died.

Paranton Bassana, aka the Indian, who knows all about exile, persuades Edmond against leaving, once and for all. What would he understand in that land of carnage for a nutmeg, offensives for a piece of ginger? He argues that his future lies right here, on the island of Bourbon, with his daughter, whose future he entrusts to him. This time, Edmond has no more doubts.

32
EDMOND'S FATHER-IN-LAW
India, 19th century

*Worse than war, there were embraces, trade agreements, mace,
and the usual peppercorns.*

Marie-Pauline Bassana's father, Paranton, let out his first wail on the coast of Coromandel, a long plain in southern India punctuated by mosquito-infested deltas and semi-wild herds. At the close of the 17th century, a ship looking neither like a Chinese junk, nor an Arabian dhow had arrived there. The captain had planted a flag in the black sand, asked where the clove trees were, cited Jean-Baptiste Colbert, and then had Louis XIV's coat of arms carved at the entrance to fishing villages. One after another, Surat, Pondicherry, Chandernagor, Yanaon became French property. There was no rebellion, no Indian cavalry with broad scimitars flashing in the haze. Worse than war, there were embraces, trade agreements, mace, and the usual peppercorns. And a few missionaries, a kind of cavalry, a cathedral of the Immaculate Conception, within musket range of the Hindu temples. It was outside one of the thatched-roofed houses that Paranton started to serve France as a palanquin bearer, before leaping, more or less gullibly, more or less drugged, into one of those adventurers' ships that was returning to Lorient, with a call at Bourbon on the way. Ignorant as he was, he couldn't even place Bourbon on a map, but he set sail all the same towards a new world that turns out to be barely a large island. In one pocket, a few sprigs of curry leaf, little leaves whose strong flavor would spice up his meals and remind him of his mother's masala. In the other, a statuette of Shiva to protect him from the worst.

On his new island, he signed a six-year contract and replaced

Coromandel with the Camp des Malabars, a district of Saint-Denis between Rue Labourdonnais and the oceanfront. There were stone-cutters, brickmakers, rattan weavers, silversmiths, small-boat builders, for whom Karikal, Bengal, and the town of Daman were now but a memory dampened with tears and blood.

The Desbassayns and other landowners acted together. They had a great many hard-working Indians brought over, got temples built for them, and made some substantial orders: three hundred kilos of rice, fifty-odd tam-tams, and floral garlands, the *maalais,* in mosaic colors. Thirty-five boxes of earplugs, too, in anticipation of the four days in January when, for the Pongal festival,[37] the menials would mistake Barachois for Tamil Nadu. It was during this very celebration that Paranton and Françoise Avallon, a young Creole woman, had met. From Saint-Denis they had moved to Commune-Carron, a district of Sainte-Suzanne where cane, coffee, and vanilla growers were always sought. Nine months later, a baby was born. On an almost mystical impulse, they named her Lakshmi, after the wife of the God Vishnu, which a registrar, out of Christian restraint, changed to Marie-Pauline Bassana.

[37] Harvest festival in the Hindu calendar. It also marks the end of the sugarcane harvest in La Réunion.

33

THE WEDDING OF EDMOND AND MARIE-PAULINE BASSANA
Green room, 1871

Love is but death simpering.

After the long period of mourning, so long that the calendar now shows 1871, when Edmond invites Marie-Pauline to meet him in the church of Sainte-Suzanne, she says yes. It was predictable as rain, a blatant lie, old as the world: they would live an unremarkable love story, dream of two or three children, then go through the gate of those who die without receiving their due of happiness. But they gave in to temptation all the same. The dream of utopian bliss, despite the permanent hell. And so, to Edmond's request to meet, and then to his marriage proposal, Marie-Pauline doesn't say no.

Between them, it began that way. Under the cleaver of hope, leaning against the chink in a wall where wallflowers grow. With the blessing of a Singer sewing machine and a deceased mother. With a touch of defiance, too, the way an arum lily grows on the side of a volcano. Just to see whether the lava will divide in two to avoid the roots. They hoped that love would succeed where freedom had failed, now there was a chance their children wouldn't get snarled on the barbed wire of slavery. At the end of a summer mellow as the dawn, they promised to wed without a marriage contract or anything fancy.

On May 11, 1871, in the presence of eleven guests, Edmond fears he might faint, as if that new machine invented by Singer were punching three hundred holes a minute in his bursting heart. He says yes to Marie-Pauline, whom he marries as their eyes turn towards the same skylight, from which a golden light falls. He is forty-two, she is twenty. It's nine in the morning. It's still summer, and the sun dazzles Edmond, who shields his eyes with the handkerchief Marie-Pauline stitched for him. Around them are gathered modest folks, people who have looked tired and ill for three generations. There's Denis Coly and Arthur Bressa, both builders, and their wives; Paul Répot, thirty-nine years old, a wheelwright, and his wife; Amédée Mably, forty-six, a grower, with his daughter; and Paranton and Simon, who, for the occasion, is wearing a scarf tied around his neck because, on the lithograph, Edmond is wearing one and it doesn't look half bad. Isidore is there, too; he wouldn't miss the wedding feast for anything in the world.

There are no speeches at the large table decorated with ferns, no great festivity. There is mainly Marie-Pauline, at all of twenty, who is clutching a white bouquet of *épis de la Vierge*[38] and wondering whether the night to come will be the most surprising of her life, as her friends have warned her.

We can picture her, slender in her white dress that covers her knees, orange blossom in her finely braided hair, eyes as dark as her skin. It's the only sunny day of the week and Edmond sees that as a sign from all of his dead, more numerous than the living, who are supporting him: his mother, his father, Ferréol, Elvire, Françoise Avallon. Between him and happiness there's always been a safe distance, a kind of mad rush towards opposing tropics, but Edmond senses that all that is behind him, and that, in this sun-soaked land, he will get his share of blue sky from now on. He goes to bed with Marie-Pauline once they've said their prayers, both shamefaced as children caught with their fingers in the pot of jam.

About their wedding night, not a rumor survives, except that in the early hours, the crucifix hung above their bed was found to be upside down.

---

[38] Stars of Bethlehem.

Since getting married, Edmond shares, with Marie-Pauline, Simon, and his father-in-law, a quarter of a plot of land bought by Paranton with his salary as an *engagé* when it reached thirty francs a month. In the neighborhood known as the Quartier-Français, they live in a cottage surrounded by chickens and giant *badamier* trees, under which they drink coffee that they mill themselves. They live meagerly on rice, what they dig up from the earth, and endless haggling for a kilo of meat and a bar of chocolate. It's but a blend of sugar and cocoa poured into a mold, but Marie-Pauline loves it so much that all three of them go to great lengths to find her some, wrapping it in newspaper and then a lace handkerchief to present it to her on the first Sunday of every month.

Five years fly by like five months, years of daily toil, small family pleasures, and great tranquility at the edge of a field planted with corn and pumpkins, and with sugarcane as far as the eye can see. Edmond lives in a house with no lock, in the midst of a herd of cows and some kid goats, which he rounds up in the evening by whistling. This hectare of contented love is so new to him that he asks for no more, expects nothing more of the world around him. Every morning, he sets off to dig, to fish, going from the house to the river, from the church to the market, from the shade to Marie-Pauline's dazzling skin. He has a father-in-law, a brother-in-law, a spouse he calls *mon ti madame, mon vie*—my wife, my life—in short, he has a family. Him, Edmond, a family! It's unhoped-for, unexpected, so remarkable! And he remembers the distant words of a *devinèr*, who had told him that an unexpected and remarkable future would find him, by hook or by crook, like the dog that, somehow, unravels conflicting scents, tackles forests, the elements, and ravines, to find, unswervingly, his master's house.

At the table, there are four of them, but they often lay it for three more: Isidore, who has a child with a Madagascan woman, never eats as well as he does in the places he invites himself to.

Every evening, in the Albius household, there rises, along with the steam from the soup, a slight tipsiness, a simple, tender, sweet contentment that tickles their hearts. They drink with a feeling of ease, play cards, tell cock-and-bull stories, and wish each other goodnight in a tone at once grateful and playful.

At night, while gazing at the blackness of her hips, her vernal navel, Edmond discovers a new landscape on Marie-Pauline's skin, of desires, of jostling yearnings he barely suspected existed. Edmond rises up from among the earthworms, and realizes that he'd needed to be close to a woman to be a man. For the first time, he understands that his father and mother, despite their wretched lives, had wanted something to be born from their almost nothing.

Edmond is forty-four and has a family.

Edmond is forty-five and drifts on a lake of peaceful routine.

Edmond is forty-six and doesn't say his prayers anymore because, when one is happy, one rarely remembers God's name.

That's it, he has his fierce victory over the world! That's it, he's found his rare fruit!

One evening, Edmond drifts off with his hands resting on Marie-Pauline, whose belly has been swelling for a few months. She would like a son, he a daughter they would name Mélise Marie Elvire. Outside, a sweeping star-dotted sky covers their little patch of paradise like a canopy. It has given them sweet rains, light clouds, such clement and calm weather for the past five years that they forget the great cyclones of old. It's a pleasant life on the plain. Edmond and Marie are both thinking that soon, upon waking, there will be three of them.

And yet, of their cliffside coupling, nothing will be born. On January 18, 1876, Marie-Pauline writes a will, and Edmond fears what lies behind it. Despite all the Earth's herbs, all the infusions of cinnamon and cherry-tree leaves, and of orange peel laced with rum and many prayers, she shivers with fever, has stopped eating, and is wasting away before his very eyes. Edmond races from forests to *devinèrs* to healers. The orchid garden is now but an overgrown jungle, the overripe vanilla pods crack, drop, wither on the ground. Edmond tramples on them without seeing them, runs on the sticky earth as fast as he can, his eyes moist and beseeching, in search of any root, leaf, flower, bark that might prove the ultimate remedy. He will bring an entire forest to Marie-Pauline if necessary.

It won't be necessary.

On January 29, 1876, less than five years since their wedding, eleven days since she wrote down her last wishes, Marie-Pauline, sick in body but not of mind, memory sharp, totally lucid, dies of fever in a land of smallpox, cholera, and endemic malediction. It's five in the morning, the cock doesn't crow. A howl of grief pierces the dawn in the Quartier-Français. It's Edmond, on whom a dark and tenacious night quietly descends. He is forty-seven years old, with no more summers to come.

What on earth did he do for everything to end like this?

In the silence of the gray morning after, rolling up the sleeves of their shirts made from heavy cotton sheets, Simon and Paranton lift Marie-Pauline's body, while Edmond is supported by his friends, who won't let him collapse. The lifeless Marie-Pauline is placed into a cart, around which the flies start to dance. Simon, acting as hearse driver, untethers his horse and sets off, with Edmond slumped beside him. The air is fresh, odorless; a light facing wind blows; the tinkling of the bells on the harness is barely audible, while the horse placidly advances, indifferent to the dead body it is carrying, to its story, to its drama.

A small group of men dressed in white leave Bellevue, Quartier-Français, and Commune-Carron at the same time. They are Edmond's friends, who all attended his wedding: his cousin, Isidore, the former neighbors of the Bassanas. Paranton leads the way down to the sea, followed by women holding palm branches. They pass the colonists' cemetery, the Malbar cemetery, and continue in the direction of a field of pebbles covered with crosses, a stone's throw from the coast. It is there that Marie-Pauline is buried, in the grave where her mother awaits her. From now on, she sleeps opposite La Marianne, a reef on which no fewer than nine schooners have been wrecked. Madame Albius's bones are cramped in a grave surrounded by pirates, voluntary *engagés*, and merchants from Bordeaux still clutching letters of marque and bogus contracts. At least Marie-Pauline will have some neighbors to talk to.

Here ends the second act of the Tragedy of Edmond Albius.

34
THE YEARS OF MOURNING
Sainte-Suzanne, 1876-1880

While, beneath the Milky Way, cyclones were pounding the walls with rage, Edmond was leading a life of utter restraint in a cottage with a creaking door.

Nothing is known of the five years that follow the death of Marie-Pauline, except that Edmond continues to live in Sainte-Suzanne. Nothing is known of his ashen life, his resigned restraint, his doubts about the goodness of the gods, his possible lost faith. Traces of Edmond are lost after the reading of his wife's will in a notary's office on June 3, 1876.

In the presence of Paranton and Simon, Edmond silently listens to her last wishes: I, Marie-Pauline, make "Monsieur Paranton Bassana, my father, residing with me, and Monsieur Edmond Albius, my husband, jointly my sole legatees; consequently, I bequeath them all the property that I will leave behind. They will enjoy and use it as they choose, having full ownership [. . .]."[39]

Gradually, Edmond tilts again towards the wrong side, that of the despairing. He smokes hemp once or twice a day, eyes half-closed, but it takes him nowhere. Outside, the months come and go, as do the cyclones. During the night of January 13-14, 1878, one cyclone devastates the island. The waves galop, growl, froth, flooding the coastal villages. From his yard, Edmond sees the roof of Sainte-Suzanne's church fly off. In Saint-André, a hospital collapses on patients, causing the death or injury of some ten *engagés*. For several hours, Edmond helps his neighbors, doing endless urgent repairs,

---

[39] Acte 10 in the Archives départementales. Will of Madame Edmond Albius, January 18, 1876.

hastily digging evacuation canals, crossing ravines, cutting down trees, reinforcing roofs that threaten to cave in. Everyone hails him as a savior, not understanding that he's doing everything he can to die.

Behind his back, the wind thrashes his mango plants, which, in falling, destroy his herb garden and his plot of corn. The rain drenches all the provisions he has stored in jute sacks.

Two months later, another storm hits the island and plunges Edmond into utter destitution. All he has left is capsicum plants—chili pepper, habanero pepper, cherry pepper—which he adds to some white rice and a fried egg for his only meal of the day. Across the island, malaria and cholera are rife. Then a fungus destroys his young coffee-tree seedlings.

Yet Edmond gets a grip on himself. His mother forbids him to die. What, is this minor hiccup going to crush him?

And so Edmond overcomes all the misfortunes, clears all the obstacles with the same fortitude, the same cheerfulness as if he were twelve with a great future. Using bits of dry wood, fallen branches, he makes stakes for his roses, supports for his maidenhair ferns.

The weeks go by, his garden grows green once more. Soon, a strange army of orchids returns there, leaning on little bamboo props, stalks supported by a brace made of string and banana fiber.

Elsewhere on the island, construction work begins for a port at the mouth of the Rivière des Galets, and a railroad line to link Saint-Benoît and Saint-Pierre. With bundles on their backs, all the vagrants who still feel strong enough to work leave the towns of the Côte-au-Vent, Saint-André, Sainte-Suzanne, Sainte Marie for the dusty, arid, sun-baked village that will later become the Ville du Port. Fifteen thousand convicts are needed to play at being workmen in the place known as La pointe des Galets. The engineer Alexandre Lavalley is on-site.

While stroking his moustache, he promotes a Pharaonic project worthy of the Suez Canal, of which he himself supervised the works. In a speech combining a few creole words with some grand commercial ambitions, he invites all the workers to bring their small stone to the giant dyke that is to be built.

At close to fifty, Edmond still, always, wants to be useful. He'd like to go over there himself, but doesn't feel up to slogging away like he did at twenty, sleeping every night in a straw hut he'll have built himself. And anyway, who would look after Paranton?

In the evening, sitting on a small wooden bench, he becomes lost in thought. His father-in-law is unaware of the nature of those thoughts. With chin and cheek resting in the hollow of his right hand, Edmond relapses into bouts of intractable melancholy. Perhaps he starts to doubt the validity of the factories, the value of the Negro sacrifice, the inept predictions of two-bit *devinèrs*. Perhaps he starts to doubt ever having a destiny. For a whole week, he barely does or says a thing. For a whole week, he expresses himself only with profanities and swearwords. The rice burns and sticks to the bottom of the pot, the pigeons are oversalted, the *sosso-maïs* is indigestible. Paranton grimaces as he gets his inedible grub down, and prays that the storm passes quickly.

The following week, Edmond regrets his wasted bitterness, his bad-loser conduct. His optimism returns, he gets his drive back. He only has a shred of family left, but he still has his memories and an iron constitution. And so he gets back in the saddle. He's up at five in the morning, prepares the sausage stew just as Paranton likes it, goes to do the weeding at *mamzelle* Jeanne's, swaps a quart of capsicums for some beans, talks to all his orchids. Things are picking up, he believes. His parents didn't bring him into the world for nothing. In two months' time, the vanilla season starts. There will be around fifty flowers to pollinate on his plot of land. For now, he awaits with confidence the reply to an umpteenth request for state remuneration, which, he doesn't yet know, he will never obtain.

Edmond comes down with just a slight fever at the beginning of August 1880. So slight, he's barely aware of it. So trifling, he's determined to keep going. He has sweet potato, chayote, pumpkin and passion-fruit creepers to water. A temperature up one degree won't finish him off. Indeed, when it comes to public health, the journalists at the *Moniteur de l'île Bourbon* write that it is good in August 1880. Apart from the seasonal flu, no epidemic is spreading. And yet, one day, on the riverbank, as he's casting his ledger line, Edmond is wracked with shivers that chill him to the bone.

"Damn!" he spits out, onto the ground, along with a large blood clot.

Edmond walks back home with a heavy step. Shaking with fever, he takes to his bed. Just for a moment, just for an hour, which turns into two days. Yes, but in two or three days, he'll be better. He pictures himself as a centenarian, like the tamarind tree lording it at the bottom of Ferréol's orchard. He'll have been mistreated by life, for sure, but he'll have had a long life, and not that sad a life, in the end. And then, next year, there'll be that giant caterpillar that's going to transport passengers and bales of vanilla from one part of the island to another. This confounded optimist wouldn't miss the launching of that for anything in the world.

35

THE END OF EDMOND
The Sainte-Suzanne hospice

Thus passes the glory of the world.

When we pick up the traces of Edmond again, it's already the second week of August 1880. A winter day, with icy drizzle, on which even Death doesn't fancy going out. Edmond is neither in Bellevue nor Quartier-Français, but in a bed at the community hospital of Sainte-Suzanne. He doesn't know who brought him there, doesn't know if Isidore knows he's there, has no idea how many days he's been turning his back on his orchids.

Edmond is alone in a hospice, looking back on his fifty-one years of life. He speaks to God knows which invisible confessor; perhaps his father-in-law Paranton Bassana, seventy years old, still a few months to live, worn out all over, perfectly sound of mind. Perhaps his cousin, nameless and faceless, who, before dying herself, passes on this story to others who distort it, diminish it, magnify it, exaggerate it. The version changes as time goes by, along with its tellers. They don't know, they suppose, they invent, they forget. There was once a young orphan slave who had discovered how to transform vanilla flowers into pods, at the close of a winter that wouldn't end. He enabled vanilla to spread, then died in utter destitution.

Edmond doesn't know the whole story. He doesn't know that, in the chill of this August 1880, Philogène Clérin, forty-seven, nurse, and Moutoussamy Satapin, forty-six, servant, will certify his death at the Village Desprez hospice. He has no idea that *Le Moniteur de l'île Bourbon* won't even mention his name among that month's deaths. That there will be but a brief article, not even bylined, to remind readers that "like more than one inventor, his peers, he lived in poverty and died forgotten."[40] There will be no sympathy, no tomb or funeral oration, barely the empathy of an incurable Lepervanche, the son of the other one, who, twenty years later, will recall that " fever, destitution soon had him lying on the pallet" and wonder "who can know the thoughts that preyed on the mind of the poor wretch when, stricken with sickness, shivering on his pallet, alone, dying of deprivation and penury, he contemplated the wealth of those whom his discovery had showered with gold and who had never thought of throwing him a scrap of bread."[41]

Outside, it's still the morning of August 9, 1880. Edmond's cheeks are wan, his forehead waxen, but he tries to sit up. The vanilla nursery is waiting for him. As is Paranton. Dark shadows carve deep hollows under his dulled eyes. He breathes heavily in a hospice where a nun moves around soundlessly. He still doesn't understand that there's nothing more to wait for, that he will see no train transporting cargoes of vanilla towards towns in France that don't know his name. He thinks only of survival and imminent justice, between fits of coughing. He's now but a little heap of pathetic flesh, who pisses on himself, with big, white frightened eyes, between sheets wet from the pain wracking his arms, back, legs. His urine is white, his stools green. In his shaking hands, he clutches the hands of that invisible one who doesn't speak.

"*I faut que mi lève*," he cries. I have to get up. He's in a complete sweat. "For *maman* who hopes, for Ferréol who's waiting for me, for Marie-Pauline who carries me."

It is one of those dismal days when vegetable peelings, leftover herring, beef tripe, a bowl of dirty water, get chucked out

---

[40] *Le Moniteur de l'île Bourbon*, weekly edition dated August 22, 1880.

[41] "La vanille et Edmond Albius," *La Revue agricole*, March 1918.

onto the dusty road. Edmond turns his dripping forehead towards the clouds that form shifting shadows in the sky.

Kala, slave and sorceress, leaves the crater of the volcano, crosses the Plaine des Sables through the fog. And here she is, approaching what's left of Edmond. From deep in his bed, he senses his heart wants to escape from his chest. His knees knock at the creaking of the door, at the sight of a strange shadow thrown by the bamboos behind the window. In the distance, the cry of a *fouquet*,[42] bird of sea and death, rings out. Edmond no longer knows if he's delirious, or if all this is real. He repeats the same names, Ferréol, Marie-Pauline, *maman*. When he has a moment of lucidity, he tells Colombine that all this is of no importance, that throughout his life, it's always been the same horde of drudgers, the same ant-men who dig, bury, carry seeds that become trees that become the trunks from which plant stakes and coffin planks are made. It's an island where everything dies fast, men as much as flowers. Edmond can't believe that it all ends like this. For the first time in his life, he wonders about what might come after, the mystery that, in a minute, will cease to be one. Will his story begin again, but differently? On the banks of the river, where the washerwomen rinse their linen, will a woman mourn for him? Do you remember, *ti père*, in the vanilla nursery, when I was a child, where everything began? Edmond would like to add something, but his tongue is heavy and hard as a tombstone. He answers "Mélise" to an imaginary question, like the conclusion and the continuation of everything.

In Quartier-Français, thousands of early, delicate flowers have just opened on Edmond's vanilla plants. They seem like garlands of light, decorations for some lugubrious function, on their stakes soaring up to the sky; but their fragile radiance, the

---

[42] Nocturnal black bird, endemic to La Réunion, also called *pétrel de Bourbon*.

rarity of their glossy fruit, that taste of vanilla they will leave on the tongue, none of that is important anymore. In his bed, Edmond knows that no brotherly hand, no friend will ever close his eyelids. It's Monday August 9, 1880, ten in the morning.

Edmond dies with his eyes open, like those among dead who make us wonder whether they are resting in peace.

ABOUT THE AUTHOR

Gaëlle Bélem was born in Saint-Benoît, Réunion Island. She is the author of two novels, *There's a Monster Behind the Door*, longlisted for the 2025 International Booker Prize, and *The Rarest Fruit*, winner of the Renaudot des Lycéens Prize. She lives in France.